The Source Stories: Book One

From the Cave Wall:

A Stone Age Story

JG Jones

First paperback edition July 2019

Book cover by D Jones

www.jgjbooks.com

Contents

Author's Note

13,000 years ago, the world was very different from the way it is now. This was the Upper Paleolithic period and our human ancestors (homo sapiens) lived in groups called bands which would contain four or five different families or households. It was vital that these people worked together to survive within the natural world. There was no electricity, cars or even permanent houses and everything came from the land around them - food, clothing and shelter.

The people of this time didn't look much different from you, but you wouldn't be able to understand their language and they mostly communicated using gestures and movements. To help tell the story, Osha and her family all use modern language that you might use today. Everything else in this book is based on historical evidence and gives an account of her life, that could be true.

Chapter One

There it was, on the top part of the wall, high out of Osha's reach: The best and most special cave painting of them all, Grandpa's painting. The torch highlighted sweeping charcoal lines which formed a simple shape, but it was the detail of the fine hairs and length of its strong tusks that impressed her. It felt to her like the eye of the great beast was looking deep inside her and she in turn was able to see within it.

With one hand gripping the flaming torch, she reached out a small finger and traced the long trunk in the air, imagining the feel of the thick leather and the size of the huge creature. The unseeing eye still stared down at her as she imagined expertly using the thick hair on its back to climb up and ride into the grasses, following the river far away from here. Together they would live out the stories her grandpa told, fighting fierce wolves and giant cave lions, racing across the land, tearing down trees and rescuing anyone in need. She was Osha the Fearless, and no one could stop her and her mammoth.

The uncertain flicker of her flame drew her attention back to where she was. She shivered as the cold of the damp cave began to eat at her exposed arms and legs. She wasn't exactly dressed for a long exploration of the caves; her simple reindeer hide tunic and leggings were made for the warm weather. Stamping her feet and moving her free fingers, she decided it was probably time to head back to the camp, her longing for the adventures of Osha the Fearless would have to wait another day.

She turned to say goodbye to her mammoth, the bravery of her dreams slipping as she thought about the row that would be had once she got back. She placed her free hand on her growling stomach and made her way back towards the entrance of the cave. Images of Ma's red face and the thought of rough tears made the growling worse. She nibbled on her dry lips and clutched the torch tightly as she thought about what she might say once she was back at the camp.

"Sorry, might be a good idea." She whispered. The words echoed in the silence, as if the walls were agreeing with her. "I didn't mean to." was another idea she had, and the ibex, rabbits and oxen agreed.

In some ways, she knew it didn't really matter what she said, Ma would be upset and angry because that was how she always was. Osha tried her best to do what she was asked to, but it was hard when the woods were perfect for running in and the caves exciting to explore. Ideas would come into her head and she would do them, even if she was meant to be collecting berries or nuts or sticks. She couldn't help it, that's just the way she was.

She sighed causing the flame of her torch to flicker even more. *Oh no*, she thought, as she was cloaked in thick darkness. She shivered as the damp walls seeped into her. She could hear the trickle of water along the wet and rocky floor. *What am I going to do now?* She no longer felt like a legendary mammoth-rider. Dropping the useless torch to the floor, she reached out for the wall beside her. *I can follow it to the entrance.*

Placing two small hands against the damp surface, she focused on her footing. Her steps were slow, and she knew that it would take her much longer than normal to get there. She shivered, once again wishing she had worn thicker clothing.

She continued walking, using the wall as her guide for a while, stopping every now and then to feel for obstacles in her path. Eventually, a speck of light up ahead brought with it a cool breeze and several stray hairs tickled her nose and mouth. "Achoo!" the sound bounced off wall, ceiling and floor as Osha hit the hard, soggy ground. Taking a deep breath, she scrubbed at her dirty, damp face and licked the coppery taste from her lip. *I just want to get back home*, she thought. With one sore hand she reached again for the wall, painfully bent her soaked knees and eased herself back up before continuing.

The speck of light got bigger and she could make out the line of trees that surrounded the cave and the path home. She removed her hand from the wall under the watchful gaze of a silhouetted bird. It cocked its head to one side, hopping away as she got too close before flying into the afternoon sky.

Blinking in the light, she savoured the fresh smell of the late summer air, a stark contrast to the musty damp of the cave. The sun was close to setting and the sky was a magnificent landscape of reds and oranges. Up on the hill above their camp, shadows of trees created a natural barrier between her band's lands and the wilderness beyond.

She looked down at the result of her tumble. *What's Ma going to say now?* She grimaced as she took in her torn, wet clothes and injured knees. Her hands had several grazes across the palms and she could again feel a trickle of blood from her lip. Rubbing her eyes, she turned towards the well-worn path and began to trudge home.

It wasn't a long journey from the cave to the campsite. As Osha walked, she noted the silence of the trees escorting her back. The birds' voices had quieted for the day and the sun's descent cloaked the path she trod. Each step she took cracked twigs beneath her and her stomach's growling was heavy and louder.

Up ahead she could hear the voices of her family. The shrill cry of her little brother Korto was comforted by a soft female voice, not any older than hers. *Pira.* Osha smiled as the familiar scene came into view. Her cousin was sat on the ground at the entrance to the camp rolling stones towards the little boy. She looked up as Osha ran to her.

"Osha! Where have you been and what happened to you? Your ma's not happy!" her voice dropped and eyes grew wide as Osha felt a firm hand on her shoulder. Pira's attention switched back to the little boy.

"No. She's not happy!" a voice behind her agreed. Osha turned to face the angry woman. Ma's hand moved from her daughter's shoulder to her own hip as she waited for an answer, with raised eyebrows and pursed lips.

"I...I'm sorry Ma." Osha said. Her shoes were suddenly very interesting and she could feel her eyes betraying her.

Ma sighed, "I ask you to do one thing, Osha. One thing. All you had to do was help. I turn my back for no time at all and you choose to run off. How is that helping me?" Her voice was growing in volume. Osha continued to stare at the stitching on her shoes.

"Look at me when I speak, Osha!" The young girl raised her head to face her. Her ma's face was even redder than usual and the lines around her eyes were deep. The dark hair that was often pulled back from her face was free and cast a crazed bush around her. She was not much taller than Osha, but she stood over her daughter like a threatening bear roaring out all her frustration at the younger girl,

"You are eight winters old, Osha. Your sister has left, your brother is off hunting every day and your p…" she stopped momentarily, swallowed and continued in a quieter but somehow more menacing tone. "I need help." Her dark eyes bore into Osha's and she could see her frustration masking something else. Korto, toddled over to them and grabbed at Ma's hand, who looked down briefly, before quickly swinging him up to rest on her hip. With another sigh, Ma took a step back and ran a shaky hand through her hair, "It is nearly about time we started getting ready for the next winter. You have to learn!" Osha nodded.

This was not the first time she had heard about her growing responsibilities. She knew that she needed to help her ma and it wasn't that she didn't want to, it was just not fun to wash hides, make clothes or gather things from the woods. Pira was lucky she enjoyed these things, mostly, and her ma and pa let her choose what she wanted to do. *Ma just yells and expects me to do as she says!* Not that she was going to say that to Ma.

Eventually the shouting stopped, and her ma closed her eyes while rubbing her forehead with a rough hand, "I just need you to help me Osha. Just help me." She sighed, pushing her hand back through her hair, before turning away. Osha reached out her left hand to her, "I'm sorry, Ma. I'll try..." but she'd walked away.

Osha sighed, turned to face Pira and helped her cousin up. "Ouch!" she exclaimed. She had forgotten the grazes that criss-crossed her left palm.

Pira let go of her hand and turned it over. "What happened, Osha? We need to show Ma." her soft voice and gentle hands led her over to the small hide tent where Osha's aunt Cosa was busy preparing spinach leaves for cooking. The tall woman took one look at Osha and the state she was in and pulled her into her arms. "What happened to you, Osha?" she said, embracing the young girl. Exhausted and overwhelmed, Osha could no longer hold back the tears.

Chapter Two

Once she had cried out all her frustration and pain, all Osha was left with were sore eyes and a damp face. She pulled away from her aunt's embrace, brushed her hair from her eyes and looked up into the concerned face above her. "I'm sorry." She said, forcing a smile and coughing to clear her throat. Her aunt's answering look of concern was almost too much, she blinked, screwed up her eyes and turned away.

"There's nothing for you to be sorry for, Osha," Her aunt said, placing a reassuring hand on her shoulder, "We all need to cry sometimes." As she said this, she covered her eyes with her hands, before dropping the gesture once again. Osha nodded in response.

"Now," her aunt continued, "let's have a look at those hands."

A short time later, once her injuries had been cleaned and her hands wrapped in thin hide bandages, she began to feel a lot better. *I wish I hadn't cried though*, she thought looking at Cosa, who had returned to separating spinach leaves. Osha stared at the damaged leggings in her lap, sighing as she was forced to rethread the bone needle for a fourth time. She glanced sideways at Pira's neat stitching, wishing her own work could look quite so effortless.

"Awoowa! Awoowa!" Osha and Pira dropped their work and grinned at each other, before scrambling to their feet and running outside the tent. In the distance, just on the edge of the camp a small group of people could be made out. The two girls stood on their tiptoes, waving at the approaching group,

"Awaawo! Awaawo!" they called back giggling at the strange words, before racing to meet the returning hunters.

"What did you get?" Osha looked from her uncle to her grandpa. Between them and her brother, Polto, they carried some fish, a large deer and several birds. Her eyes lit up when she noticed a particular addition to their food resources. Grandpa smiled, his green eyes twinkling,

"Not a lot I'm afraid. Certainly nothing that a little girl could possibly want." he laughed as Osha pulled on his arm.

"Let me see, Grampa! Please!" He gave up the pretence and showed off the catch of the day. The two girls gasped, "It's huge!" Pira said. The fish was a large salmon.

"Yes. It wasn't an easy one to get." Grandpa nodded. "Now, we need to prepare it for our meal. You girls can help, you need to learn this! Usso, Polto, put the rest of the spoils within the store." Osha's uncle and brother nodded before adjusting their loads and splitting off from the group.

"Can I carry it, Grampa?" Osha asked, but the old man shook his head, the fading light, reflecting in his eyes, "Not this time, Young'un. It's a heavy one." Osha thought she probably could have carried it, but she knew not to argue with Grandpa. He was the leader of the band and what he said was listened to. Always.

They made their way to the large rock where food was prepared, close to the family hearth, for ease when cooking. Between the three of them they lifted the large fish onto the stony surface.

"Thank you," Osha whispered to the unseeing fish as it lay before them and felt an approving hand on her shoulder, before the old man knelt beside it, his knees creaking as he lowered himself. Beckoning to both the girls, he picked up a flint tool and held it out to them. It was a flat, long and wide shard of flint which had been sharpened into a point,

"This is your gutting knife. See the edge is nice and sharp, so we can get a good clean cut?" Osha nodded. The edges were very narrow and the tip of the blade was sharp enough to slice her finger open. "Now then, we hold the blade like this," He said, tucking his fingers safely away from the blade. "Place your other hand on the top of the fish in the middle, like this."

As he did so, he positioned the edge of his blade at the base of the salmon's tail and, in one swift motion, sliced through the thick flesh of the fish. Then using a piece of flat reindeer antler, as well as the blade, he began cutting and scooping out the insides. The girls winced slightly as the wet and smelly fish guts squelched into the waiting bowl. Osha was pleased these wouldn't be eaten, but be thrown back into the river, to feed other creatures who lived in the water.

Grandpa chuckled at their reaction, as he wiped his fish-covered hands on a scrap piece of hide. "Ah can't beat the smell of fish gutting!" he said, watching their grimaces. He liked to tease but knew it was important they learn, "See, nice and easy."

"Mmmm, there's nothing in the world like the smell of fish guts!" A laughing voice declared as Uncle Usso came up behind them. "Cosa will take the job from here, Pa." he said, helping Grandpa off the ground.

The older man gripped his son's hand as he slowly stood and nodded. "I must go and sit down. That fishing has tired me out." They watched as he disappeared inside the sleeping tent.

"Pira, go let your ma know the fish is ready." Usso said, turning to his daughter, "I am going to speak to Osha for a moment." As he brought a hand to his mouth in the common gesture for 'speak', he smiled. The young girl

17

nodded and skipped off to her ma. Osha picked up the knives Grandpa had used, wiped them and placed them out of the way. "Osha." She felt the gentle hand of her uncle on her shoulder and turned to face him, "Your aunt told me what happened before," his green eyes, so like his own pa's, were full of concern. Osha looked away and he let go of her shoulder, "If you don't want to talk, that's fine. Just know…" he stopped and she glanced back again, curious as to what he might say next, "Just know that your ma doesn't mean to upset you. Things are hard for her, ever since…" he stopped and shook his head.

"Since what?" Osha said, frowning. He didn't answer but continued to shake his head.

"Things are just hard for her. That's all I can say." He gave her a sad smile and squeezed her shoulder before turning away again. "Now, the young ones need to be ready for the meal. Go and help Pira." He said as he walked back towards the hearth.

Osha sighed, brushing her hair out of her face. She watched her uncle gather a pile of sticks and drop them beside the gently smouldering fire. *Nobody ever tells me anything!* She thought of the dream she had had only a while earlier, of riding off on her mammoth. *That wouldn't help.* She pushed a hand through her messy hair and went to find Pira.

The delicious aroma of gently roasting salmon wafted through the camp a short while later, catching the attention of the young girls as they wrestled with their younger siblings. On entering the tent where the little ones were, Osha had attempted to apologise again to Ma who had merely looked at her, frowned and left. Pira had shrugged and shaken her head before smoothing the soft curled hair on her little sister, Lota's head. Korto, who had seen only two winters, had then toddled over to Osha and dumped a very soggy something into her lap, before giggling and bumping down in front of her.

There had followed a short time of playing and attempts, on the girls' part, at getting ready for the sundown meal. All the while Osha had thought about the events of the afternoon and her uncle's reluctance to talk to her about her ma's reaction.

"Ohwooooh!" The shrill call, which echoed around the camp, hurried them. Gathering together thick hides and wiping their faces, they gripped the hands of their younger siblings, before they made their way to the low stone seats surrounding the hearth.

The heat of the flames as they licked the piles of twigs, beneath the precious leaf-wrapped salmon, was welcome as the late summer day faded into night and the family gathered around. A cool breeze blowing around the camp, made them glad for their warm hides as they sat together, Osha making sure to sit far away from her ma.

"We thank the spirits for this salmon feast!" Grandpa declared, holding a carved wooden bowl above his head. Uncle Usso and he then gently unwrapped the salmon from its leaf blanket and Osha watched as the glorious pink fish was shared between the bowls of spinach leaves. The babies, now sitting at the feet of the women and wrapped up in thick reindeer hides, were given more spinach than salmon, but Osha grinned as she saw the large chunk of steaming fish that Grandpa handed to her. Conversation died down as everyone tucked into their meal, the hot fish and delicious salad leaves filling their hungry bellies.

Once the bowls were empty and had been gathered in, conversation began again, as fingers where licked clean. Osha and Pira took their normal position, sitting on the floor close the hearth as Osha told her about her adventure in the cave.

"You have to be careful, Osha," her cousin said, tenderly unwrapping and inspecting the wounds on her cousin's hands. Osha grinned at her, "It didn't hurt too much! I don't want to try walking in there without a torch again, though." She said, telling her how she'd accidentally blown out the flame. The memory made her laugh and Pira joined in.

"What are you two laughing at?" the curious voice of her uncle cut through their giggling.

"Osha was just telling me what happened in the cave." Pira replied to her father.

"Oh, that cave!" a stern voice said and Osha stopped giggling almost immediately. "I should stop you going to that cave at all." Her ma declared, glaring at her daughter. Osha noticed that she wasn't sitting in her usual place between Aunt Cosa and Grandpa, instead she had found a spot furthest out from all of them. Her dark eyes reflected in the flame and added to her air of anger.

"Mara! That's enough. Osha has said sorry and it is left there. She will not be going there unless she had done all that she is asked." The commanding voice of Grandpa stopped her ma from saying more.

Instead she turned to address Aunt Cosa, "Fine. I will take the children to bed." She thrust out a hand for Lota and Korto, who oblivious to the tension in the air, happily stood before being marched towards the sleeping tent. Osha swallowed, she had seen Ma angry and frustrated before but never like this. The image of the mammoth once again formed in her head, she could see his long tusks, his kind eye and the detail on his back. The idea that she might not see him again…she couldn't bear it.

"I think it is time for a tale." A voice broke into her musings, "Osha was in the cave, once again looking at my mammoth. Is that five times this moon cycle?" Grandpa smiled as he teased, breaking the tension of Ma's abrupt departure.

Osha smiled through threatening tears and nodded, "Five and a bit. Last time I was in the cave, but you called me back."

He laughed as he stood, his arms beckoning the family to draw nearer, "Well as always your love of the mighty mammoth will feed this night's tale."

The girls grasped each other's hands and pulled their hide blanket tighter around their shoulders. Grandpa's tales were legendary: The tale of the brave band member who used fire to scare off a cave bear; the legend of the powerful warrior who took down multiple wolves with only a spear when the safety of his household was threatened.

These stories were old ones and had probably changed over the years of being told. Her family had recorded events through pictures on the walls of the cave for many, many years, the natural canvas telling their story. Grandpa's knowledge of the pictures had been passed down from his family, who had in turn heard them from their family. This tradition of oral history enabled the important lessons to be learned many years after they had taken place.

Osha's favourite though, like with the mammoth painting, were when Grandpa told stories about himself. She could imagine him as a young man, not much older than her older brother, his long auburn hair glinting in the sunlight, a spear resting in his hand and his powerful legs driving him through the grasslands.

"I think this night, as my young granddaughter loves it so much, I will tell the tale of my first mammoth hunt. The first time I saw a mammoth."

Osha's eyes widened, this was not a story she had heard before. She snuggled down in her blanket, her eyes trained on her grandpa. The family around the hearth were silent as he began his tale.

"Many, many seasons ago, when I was a small boy, not much beyond your own winters in age, I saw my first mammoth." He declared grandly, sweeping his hands down and away from his face, in the rarely used gesture for mammoth.

"My pa had sent me out to gather berries from the woods. I was a good boy and did what my pa said." His eyes rested on Osha for a minute, a smile playing at his lips. She hid her face, giggling as she knew this was far from the truth.

He continued, "It was as I was coming back to the camp, my basket (and belly) heavy with fruit, that I heard the strangest of sounds." He stopped, put his hands to his mouth with his thumb resting underneath his chin and called "Maroo! Maroo! Maroo!" The unusual call echoed around the camp and Grandpa waited for it to stop before continuing,

"I had not heard that call before and as I got to the edge of the camp, my pa ran up to me, grabbed me by the hand and pulled me out towards the grasslands, just over there in fact." Grandpa pointed out beyond the trees,

"We stood looking out into the wilds and before long were joined by many other people. Not just from our band, neither, there were people I had never seen before. That call, you see, is passed from one band to another, there must have been forty people standing around.

We watched as the giant beasts crashed through nearby trees. Then all sprang into action. My pa held me back from joining in but let me watch. Groups of people stood around at different points. In their hands they held their spears, high above their heads ready to throw. Then they ran. One person after another, chasing the mammoth. Running him off. Running him towards the cliffs.

I remember my pa's arm holding me still, I wanted to be there, be one of those runners. Be a part of the hunt. I followed them in my mind as they disappeared from view, continuing to chase. A cheer was passed from band to band as the beast was felled. The meat was shared between all who took part. I made it my dream that day, to one day join in that hunt." Grandpa stopped, smiling sadly as the memories of his youth receded. For a minute in the firelight, Osha thought, he had looked ten winters younger, his eyes sparkling and his hands moving from one well known gesture to another.

"You did, Pa. The cave painting tells us so." Uncle Usso, helped his pa sit down beside him, pulling up a warmed hide from the ground near the hearth and wrapping it around the old man's shoulders.

"I did, aye," the old man sighed, taking a stick to poke the fire as he stared into the flames "but now, we haven't seen a mammoth in many winters." It suddenly felt far colder as the late evening closed in around them.

"Do you think we will ever see a mammoth, Grampa?" Osha said, moving to sit beside him. He put an arm around her shoulder and pulled her into his side.

"I hope so, Young'un, I really do. They are wondrous beasts. I know you hold my picture in your heart but...to see one, Young'un..." He looked down at her upturned face and stroked her hair while shaking his head, "It is the better than that."

The image of her riding her mammoth came into her mind and she shook her head. "I'm going to see one, Grampa. And not only see one, I'm going to ride one!"

The old man laughed, "He might not let you, Young'un." He said, before taking her small hand in his and placing it gently over her heart,

"But by the help of the spirits, I hope you do."

Chapter Three

The next morning dawned with a warm sun but accompanied by a strong cool wind that blew the outside coverings of the tents in the camp and rocked the wooden poles which kept it aloft. Swirling around the tent, it tickled the face of a sleeping Osha, who was deep in dreams of mammoths; riding in the wilderness and taking lessons from a young man who looked like her older brother, Polto but wasn't him.

As her mammoth blew a gentle breath on her face, she opened her eyes and realised where she was. Tiny pin-pricks of light had invaded through the seams and joins of the stretched animal hide, breaking the pitch darkness of the tent.

She pulled the soft reindeer skin blanket up, closer to face blocking out the light and sudden chill. Turning her head, she saw that the other sleeping mats, around her and the slumbering Pira, were empty. Her brother and uncle must have woken up early to go hunting. Grandpa too was nowhere to be seen and outside, she could hear the quiet murmur of voices which meant that Ma and Aunt Cosa were awake and preparing the morning meal. Small, high-pitched squeaks and giggles told her that the youngest members were also awake and playing together.

While Pira still snored quietly beside her, Osha blinked and sat up, pulling the blanket to cover her bent knees and thought about her dream and the story Grandpa had told the night before. He had been so lucky. She closed her eyes, put her head on her knees and grasped her hands to her heart.

*By the spirits and their wisdom, I will see a mammoth. I will see a mammoth. I **will** see a mammoth.* She repeated to herself, once again seeing the image of Grandpa's mammoth, except this time she stood beside him, staring into his beautiful eyes and watching the soft breeze waft through the long hair covering his impressive head.

"Osha! Pira!" Osha's daydream disappeared as her eyes snapped open. She lifted her head to see her aunt's smiling face peering around the edge of the sleeping tent. "It's time to get up, girls. The spirits have greeted us with a lovely day and we have the last of the berries ready for the morning meal. So, come on, we have a job for you to do."

With a final smile, Aunt Cosa disappeared. Osha reluctantly stretched her sleep-heavy limbs, yawned and looked over at the still snoozing girl beside her. Dark hair covered Pira's face and long freckled arms were flung out either side of her. She looked so peaceful that Osha was loath to wake her. She lightly shook the younger girl's shoulder, afraid to startle her,

"Pira. Pira, it's time to wake up." She whispered. Very slowly and sleepily, Pira opened her emerald eyes and smiled.

The promised berries were waiting for them, as the sleepy girls emerged from their tent. Ma and Aunt Cosa were chatting quietly together, Ma showing a rare lightness and smiling at her brother's partner, as Pira and Osha sat down.

Ma looked up and handed them their bowls of food, before placing a willow basket down on the ground in front of them,

"Girls, when you've finished eating, I need you to go into the woods and find some more berries. Our store is running low," She looked pointedly at her daughter, "Remember Osha, no getting distracted by the cave or anything else." Osha nodded, placing another juicy berry in her mouth and smiling,

"Yes Ma. I will only look for berries." She said, inspecting the bowl and taking time to pick out the juiciest and reddest berries first.

"Good girl." Ma said smiling and wiping her hands, she indicated for her to sit in front of her. Osha sat down with the bowl in her lap and Ma gently started trying to tame the wild hair on her head. Osha loved the feel of her ma's fingers gently teasing the knots, smoothing the strands as best she could and tenderly braiding the crazed mop.

Her uncle walking past their small group, briefly kissing her aunt's cheek and giving her cousin a quick morning hug, made her think of the strange man in her dream,

"...He was helping me learn to ride the mammoth, Ma. It was strange, I knew him, but also didn't. He looked really like Polto, but it wasn't him." she felt the gentle hands in her hair pull away one by one and turned around. Ma's cheeks had lost their colour and her eyes had glazed over.

"Ma? Are you ok?" Osha asked, she hadn't seen her like this before. Ma blinked, shook her head and when brown eyes snapped to meet green, they were once again clear,

"I'm perfectly fine Osha. Now if you've finished your berries, you and Pira can head into the forest. No distractions remember." She snapped before standing and moving away.

Osha knew that she would not get any answer from Ma. Stuffing the last of her breakfast in her mouth, she picked up the baskets, before turning to Pira, who had been quietly chatting with her own ma and beckoning for her to follow.

During the summer months, the canopy of leaves which lined their path was so thick that very little sunlight could be seen. The vibrant green of the foliage contrasted with the looming dark and gave a strange sense to the area. Tall trees stretched as high as the clouds, casting thick shadows upon the ground, leaving you cold and shivering. These trees had vast, ancient trunks which, if you stood behind them, hid you completely from the sight of anyone on the other side.

From deep within the woods, unidentifiable shrieks and calls accompanied the eerie song of hidden birds while the whoosh of the gushing river nearby was distorted and seemed to be the strange voices of lost spirits.

Aside from the cave, this was, in Osha's opinion, the best place to be.

"Remember Pira, these woods have been a part of our family's lives for many, many winters." Osha said, a mischievous gleam in her eyes. Her cousin nodded, wary of what was to come,

"Like old Litsa, the spirit walker…" she stopped, casting her gaze around the dark-scape surrounding them. Suddenly she pointed a finger behind her, towards a thick patch of woodland, "There. Can you see, she watches us…deep in the woods."

She turned to Pira whose face did not reflect her own delight, "Stop it, Osha. You know I don't like scary stories."

With wide eyes she surveyed the area before bringing her attention back to Osha and whispering, "Anyway, you know it is dangerous to speak of the spirits in such a way." Osha rolled her eyes, but nodded in agreement, after all, she did not want to anger the spirits.

"I'm sorry, Pira" she said and just to be safe, she cast her eyes around her one more time and whispered,

"I'm sorry, Litsa."

Despite the unnerving atmosphere, these woods had truly been an essential part of hers and her many ancestors' lives. From here they had foraged for sweet treats and nuts; hunted small creatures; found sanctuary when threatened by wolves or lions. It was also a welcome haven from the rush of the camp and the outside world.

As the children walked towards the clearing where they knew certain berries were to be found, it was possible to see the different paths that many people had taken, wearing their journeys into the landscape and the story of the forest.

The girls stopped in front of a particular bush and looked at each other, "This is ok, isn't it?" Osha said, indicating the red berries that adorned the small shrub.

Pira nodded, "Yes. They are the ones we collected before." For many moon cycles, their mas had taken them into the woods, showing them which berries were safe to eat and which it was essential to avoid,

"and look, that small bird is picking at one. My ma told us that if they can eat them, we can too." At this final confirmation, they reached gentle fingers into the bush, scaring away the feeding birds.

For a long time, the girls moved through the woods from one bush to another, placing the juicy, delicious berries into their basket. Every so often, they would stop and look at each other pointing to a different bush, "Is this one ok?" was a repeated question which was met with either a nod or a shake of the head.

With a full basket and stained fingers, they smiled at each other, "Shall we head back to camp?" Osha asked, adjusting the weight in her hands. Pira nodded and the girls prepared to leave their gathering spot.

CRACK.

The sound made them stop immediately. Pira and Osha's heads both snapped towards the sound, just in the distance.

"Shhh!" Osha placed a finger to her lips and pointed to a nearby tree with a thick trunk, a few steps away, "we need to hide behind that tree over there." she whispered in her cousin's ear.

Pira nodded, her face white and her eyes wide. Each girl gripped the other's hand as they tip-toed over to the tree.

Another sharp sound came from the same direction and the two girls quickened their pace. Osha could feel her heart pounding beneath her hide tunic. She rubbed her sweating palms against her legs and motioned to Pira to crouch down.

"I'm scared, Osha," the little girl whispered as she moved closer to her side, "what if it's a bear or a lion?" Pira's fears reflected Osha's own. She had no idea what to do if it was a predator. *Run, I guess.* She just hoped the beast wouldn't chase them.

Gently placing an arm around her shoulder, she hugged Pira to her, softly stroking the top of her arm, "It's ok Pira. I'll protect you." She knew she had to remain calm and level headed: she was the older of the two (by about a moon cycle), the leader, like Grandpa. Her voice shook slightly as she reassured Pira, but the young girl seemed to accept it.

Gulping down the horrid taste in her mouth, Osha made a decision that she hoped was the right one, "Stay here. I'm going to look." Hiding her fear from her cousin, she peered around the tree.

Crouching on the ground, in front of a bush the two girls knew to avoid, was the back of a very slim, young, dark haired boy. His feet were bare, and his dirty hair matched her own in length; down to his shoulder blades. He wore very simply made hides which appeared far too big for him, the bottoms almost hiding his feet.

Osha watched as he pushed his small hand far into the bush, took one of the berries between his thumb and finger and went to place it in his open mouth.

"STOP!" Osha screamed, as she raced towards the boy. Her wild hair flew out behind her and she failed to stop herself before knocking him over into the mud.

"Gerroff me!" He grunted as he wrestled himself away from her, stood and brought his fists up. Osha jumped back, her own fists ready.

The boy's grey eyes momentarily flicked his attention towards the ground and his face fell as he took in the destruction of the snack he had been about to have.

Before either of them could react further, a small voice called from behind the tree which Osha had just left, "Is...is it safe to come out?" Osha looked at the boy and raised an eyebrow. His curiosity overtaking his sense of injustice, he turned and warily lowered his arms, looking towards the tree.

"Yeah. You're fine to come out now." Osha called back. In response, a small, frowning face timidly appeared from the back of the tree, followed shortly after by a body. She stayed glued to the trunk as she looked towards the situation in front of her.

"Who're you?" The boy grunted, pointing a finger first at Osha and then at Pira, who was gaining more confidence and edging closer to the pair, now that she knew he wasn't going to eat her!

Osha stood forward as she proudly declared herself, "I'm Osha and this is Pira. We're from the household near the cave. Who're you?" The boy looked from one girl to the other. He drew himself up tall (though he was shorter than both of them), pushed his hands through his messy hair, drawing out the sticks and leaves that had become caught when Osha ran into him, and equally proudly said,

"I'm Inko. I live over there." His hand waved in the general direction of the cave and Osha smiled, she knew Inko's household, "My sister Kita was joined to one of your lot a season ago, just after we came back from our winter camp."

She smiled at the boy, who was still looking warily at them, fidgeting with his fingers, "She's older than me but I'm better at making knives, she can never strike the flint with the hammer right." she brought her fist into her other, in the gesture for knapping and continued, "her blades are always tiny," she said, smirking and holding her left thumb and forefinger apart.

The boy's blank look wasn't encouraging so Pira, who had finally fully unstuck herself from the tree, carried on,

"But she is really good at hide-work. Look!" she said, turning around on the spot, "she made this tunic and leggings!" She stopped, realising that the boy had lost interest and was eyeing the bush again, as Osha moved to stand in front of it.

"Well I ain't ever heard of her." Inko said, shifting again to see past her. Osha, looking at Pira, shrugged. *No need to be so defensive!* Silence descended on the small group.

"So, when're you gonna tell me why you pushed me over?" demanded the surly boy. Osha had never met anyone so rude before! She frowned, shaking her head before stalking towards the smashed berries.

"These berries aren't for eating! You'll get sick! You might even die!" Her voice rose in irritation. "Hmph!" he scowled at her, "How do you know that? They're just berries, animals eat them!" Osha, beginning to think she should have left him to his fate of stomach cramps, glared at him and gritted her teeth, "How about you try them then? See what happens?"

The boy's face betrayed his uncertainty as Pira gasped and stepped forward to stop him, but he pushed past her

45

outstretched hand, marched up to the bush, shoved his hand back in and snatched a small handful of berries.

Osha pointedly watched, as he lifted his hand to his mouth. "It's really not a good idea," Pira said. His grey eyes reflected her concern, but he seemed determined to prove them wrong. In one go, he put all the berries into his mouth and chomped down.

"Urgh!" he spat, "They're disgusting!" Slimy grey juice ran down his face and onto his tunic as his tongue hung out of his mouth, not wanting to be victim to the vile taste any longer.

Pira looked around for something to help as the boy flailed around, while Osha desperately tried to keep a straight face as she watched his jumping and yelping. *Serves him right for not believing me!* She thought to herself. Her cousin reappeared with a handful of cabbage leaves and held them out to the suffering boy.

A laugh could not be stopped from exploding out of Osha when he grabbed the handful and stuffed the green leaf into his mouth before sitting down panting by the tree the girls had hidden behind, desperately chewing on the leaves.

"See?" Osha asked quietly, once she could breathe again. Inko did not look amused and he crossed his arms before returning to the deep frown that had so irritated her.

It would serve him right if we got up and left him here! She thought, then looked at Pira who was still looking concerned. *It's his own stupid fault...if he'd listened to us...* Osha sighing and rolling her eyes marched over to the basket, picked up a handful of blackberries and took them over to the still scowling boy.

"Here you go, Grumpy." The boy looked up into Osha's face, shooting daggers once again. She rolled her eyes, plucked a juicy, black berry from the basket and dramatically placed it into her mouth before throwing another to Pira, who had come up behind her.

The boy looked for a bad reaction. Finding none, he reached towards the basket and took a berry. Warily, he slowly brought his teeth together and grinned as the berry's juice exploded in his mouth, before reaching to take a handful.

Silence fell once again as the girls watched him eat then looked at each other. Once his handful was empty, Osha sat down beside him. She wasn't quite sure what to say, but she couldn't leave him to starve. His household obviously hadn't taught him about which were safe to eat, and which weren't.

She smiled at him, "Come on, Inko stick with us. We'll show you where these are, and which others are good." She didn't ask why he didn't know, some households did it differently, she guessed. He seemed to accept that they wanted to help. Pira picked up the full basket and followed her cousin and the strange boy.

"They taste much better without the cabbage first!" Osha grinned and wandered towards a bush which the girls hadn't quite picked clean.

Chapter Four

Hours later, with sticky and purple juice smeared around their faces, the girls waved goodbye to the strange young boy. They watched as he wandered off into the dark woods.

"I like him," Osha said as she turned to Pira, who was clutching the almost overflowing basket of berries. "He doesn't talk much, but I like him." She looked towards the past-midday sun and shielded her eyes. "We'd better get back. Ma'll want her berries."

Taking charge as ever, she began to march back towards the camp. Pira followed close behind carrying their precious prize. The abundance of fruit they had managed to collect was a good sign that the winter would not be as harsh as previous ones. Despite her young age, Osha could remember not long ago when they had been unable to collect food for several days. She didn't miss the gnawing belly cramps and perishing winds that chilled you to the bone, even through thick hide clothing.

Shivering at the memory, she turned to Pira, "Ma'll be happy with the basket." The younger girl nodded, adjusting it in her hands.

Osha had no idea what the problem was, but before she could ask, Ma came bustling towards them, "Well, you two took your time. When I ask you to do a job for me, I don't expect it to take all morning, or for you to come back covered in juice!" Ma's angry face was matched by her tone.

Silently, Pira handed the basket to her. She relaxed slightly as she saw it was almost overflowing. "Lucky for you that you found this much. Now, go and clean yourselves off at the river. Oh, and you might remind your Grandpa that he can't keep fishing all day, we need some more knives making, they keep disappearing!" She hurried off back towards the camp and the girls followed a safe distance behind.

A glistening strip of silver outlined by large trees was not far from their camp. It was the perfect place for fishing and Grandpa spent many hours there. As they walked, Osha's attempts to draw Pira into conversation were met only with small smiles or nods of the head. Pira wasn't a loud person but usually on days like this they told stories or laughed about something that had happened recently (usually about Grandpa). Today, something definitely wasn't right.

"You're very quiet, Pira. You ok?" she said. The little girl looked up towards her cousin and nodded,

"Yeah. I just...I was so scared in the woods Osha. What if it hadn't been Inko? What if it had been a bear or a lion? We could've been eaten! I don't want to be a bear's dinner!" The poor girl was close to tears. Osha stopped walking and put her arm around her cousin. She pulled her into her and hugged her close,

"Come on, don't cry. You're safe, you won't get eaten." Pira's water-filled eyes continued to show her concern. Osha thought for a moment before continuing,

"Anyway I know what we'd have done. We'd have made ourselves really, really big and growled at them. They'd have run away then. Look." Letting go of her cousin, Osha stood still with her arms stretched out wide, trying to make her very small shape twice the size. Her mouth open, she clenched her teeth together and growled at an imaginary predator.

"Grrrrrrrr," the noise vibrated in the back of her throat. Pira giggled at her best friend's silliness. Osha's smile lit up her face,

"You try! You stand like this, legs wide, arms wide out to the side with your fingers curled, like claws. Yeah that's right." she looked at Pira as she tried to copy,

"Then you take a deep breath, close your teeth...and...GRRRRRRRRRR!"

A shaggy greying head with matching beard appeared around a nearby tree, "Oy! What's all that noise? You young'uns are frightening the fish away!"

They had been so focused on their conversation that they hadn't even realised they'd reached the river. In front of them, stood an elderly man holding a very wet looking pole. On the end, attached by some flax, hung a very long and sharp bone hook. The girls were careful not to get in the way of the potentially vicious weapon, as they ran to greet Grandpa.

"Just you watch out there, young'uns. That's a nasty point on that one, it'll go clean through your foot!" He moved the dangerous tool out of the way,

"So what've you two been up to? No mischief, I hope? You've not been in the cave, have you?" His playful eyes, mostly directed at Osha, twinkled as he stood back from the pair.

"Nope Grandpa. We did meet a strange boy though, didn't we Pira? He was from where Kita lives now." Grandpa nodded as Osha continued, "but he didn't know her. Said he'd never even heard of her!"

She'd been pondering the conversation since leaving the woods. The more she thought about it, the stranger it became. She could understand him not knowing what Kita looked like, but it did seem strange that he didn't even recognise her name. She remembered too, that the whole household had come down to the river for a celebratory feast during the joining, but she couldn't remember seeing a young boy like Inko. On top of that, his lack of any knowledge about what it was safe to eat was very, very odd.

Grandpa himself looked puzzled, as she told him her thoughts. He frowned and seemed to be thinking about something,

"Hmmm...that is very strange Young'un. Up behind the cave, you say? Well they're not a big household, only seven or eight of them and I don't think they've got any young'uns. How old was he?"

Osha wasn't sure, she thought that he was probably a similar age to her, but he was very small, and she'd been able to topple him very easily.

"I think he's about our age," Pira piped in and Grandpa frowned again,

"Very strange." He turned away from them,

"Ah I've just remembered," he said, turning back, "the household beyond Kita's have some young'uns. Maybe you just got muddled?" This seemed like a reasonable response, Osha didn't know anyone from there. She smiled and nodded, *Grampa really does solve everything!* The old man placed his hands on his hips,

"Now, next time, please remember, noise near the river really isn't helpful when I'm fishing," he said, looking at Osha, "if you want salmon, you've got to stay quiet!"

Osha's eyes lit up, "Oooh! Salmon, Grampa? My favourite!" she said jumping up and down on her toes. Grandpa smiled and Pira giggled, her earlier concern completely forgotten.

"Well, help me carrying this all back to camp and we can get to looking at making those knives your mas have been moaning about!"

The two girls giggled at this as they followed him up towards the camp. Between them, in a large hide sling, they carried the dead fish. This would be another great addition to the band's food share. The five households in their band looked out for each other which meant that food was shared. Anything caught, killed or foraged went to the shared hearth situated between the camps.

As they reached the camp as short while later, Grandpa signalled the catch to be placed down before placing his hands around his mouth and calling the returning hunters' greeting.

"Awoowa! Awoowa!" The girls joined in, giggling. Not long after, the gentle response was heard and Pira's ma appeared, one hand on her hip, while the other shielded her eyes from the sun. Her soft, round face was lit up in a broad smile and as the group moved closer towards her, she began rolling up her sleeves of her loose tunic.

"I see the fisherman and his helpers have arrived home. Salmon again is it, Anso?" Osha always found it strange to hear people call Grandpa that name. The old man nodded in response to the question and Cosa smiled,

"It's the season, I suppose." she peered at the glassy eyed fish, "Good size though, will feed a lot of us. Let's get it on the rock and I'll sort it out." Between the four of them, they were able to lift the large fish onto the same rock which Grandpa had used the previous night.

It was a beautiful fish. About twice the length of Osha's arm, the scales glistened in the sun, the black spots along its back breaking up the endless silver. Osha's mouth watered at the thought of the juicy pink fish she would get to eat again.

"Right I'd best be sorting this fish for the food share. You girls go with Grandpa and get working on those blades. I could only find two earlier, no idea where they keep running off to." Cosa said, breaking Osha's salmon daydream. She picked up the two blades she had been able to find and ushered the children away.

Pira and Osha happily ran towards the flint-work area, Grandpa quietly said something to Cosa and followed behind at a more sensible pace,

"Slow down young'uns you don't want to slip, this area is covered in shards!" His warning did little to slow them down, but they did keep their eyes on the ground.

The blade-work section of the camp was towards the back of their land, far away from both the family hearth and tents at the front but also the line of dense forest which surrounded their home.

The girls eagerly sat as close together as possible on one of the larger rocks, waiting for Grandpa to catch up. They clutched each other's arms and giggled as the old man walked up to them, holding a pile of leathers.

"Now young'uns, you can't sit like that when you're knapping flint!" he shook his head and smiled as he handed them each a piece of leather and directed one or other to a smaller rock not far away. In turn, he took the rock in the middle, placing his own piece of leather on his lap as he did so. His tools were already laid out on the ground.

He slowly reached down, his back creaking slightly, grasped the thick hammer stone and large core piece of flint and held them up so the girls could see them. Faint silver scars on the backs of his hands were matched on the girls', they had knapped flint many times before and were ready (now on their own seats) with their leathers across their knees, their hammer and core stones in hand,

"Right, young'uns, now we're wanting some good-sized blades, so your ma doesn't complain," he said, looking at Osha, his eyes twinkling.

"Remember, strike the core with the hammer stone in just the right place and a good-sized shard should break off! The one who can make the biggest and neatest three blades will get a prize!"

At the mention of a prize, Osha immediately started focusing on the piece of flint resting on her lap. She lifted the hammer stone and listened closely as she hit the flint in different directions to make the flakes.

From time to time, Grandpa softly reminded them both to clear the debris from their legs or suggested trying a different angle, but for most of the afternoon the camp rang only with the sound of stone striking stone as the girls worked to make their blades.

As they worked, shards were examined and those deemed likely competitors set aside for Grandpa to judge. The ground at their feet became covered in flakes of all sizes and their hands grew sore, but both girls were determined to win the competition.

"Right, let's see how you've done." After hours of silence, Osha jumped at Grandpa's loud voice.

She looked at the range of blades she had in front of her. She'd managed to knap five or six good competitors. The other much smaller shards were moved out of the way. Picking each up in turn, she turned them one way and the other, examining their natural sharpness and shape. At last she chose the ones she thought were the best. Feeling confident, she handed them over to Grandpa who grinned at the girls.

His face was solemn as he picked the blades up one by one, inspecting them thoroughly. Once he had made his decision, he stood up and turned to the girls, "I do declare that today's winner is..." he paused for effect. The two girls were silent as they eagerly waited for his answer, "...PIRA!" He held up the shiny black blades before placing them on a nearby rock,

"Come and collect your prize, my dear!" he said, his arms open wide.

Pira stood, "I won?" she said, a look of shock on her face. Dazed, she ran up to Grandpa.

"Well done, my girl!" he said giving her a large bear hug. For a moment, Osha felt a surge of jealousy. Gritting her teeth, she swallowed her pride as tears threatened.

"Well done Pira!" she said, sniffing, "I'll beat you next time, though!" the grin on her cousin's face, as she ran off towards the family hearth, made the loss worth it. Osha looked at the blades sitting on the rock. Pira really had done well.

"It was a close one, Young'un." Grandpa said, placing a hand on her shoulder, "Yours were good blades, but Pira's were just slightly bigger. Your ma'll be happy though, we've got another good six blades there and I think there are some others you both knapped that we can use too."

He bent down to pick up a few that had been discarded. The sound of Pira's laughter and a loud cheer made them both look up. Beside the family hearth stood Uncle Usso with Lota on his shoulders and Aunt Cosa with one arm wrapped around him. In front of them eagerly jumping from foot to foot was Pira. Osha couldn't hear what was being said, but she could guess. She tried to ignore another surge of jealousy which ran through her.

"I made Ma angry again, Grampa. All I was doing was telling her about the man in my mammoth dream who looked like Polto but wasn't." She hoped that maybe the old man might help her work out who he was. Instead, he sighed and placed a hand on her shoulder.

"Your ma isn't angry Young'un, she's just..." he stopped and looked towards his son and his family still joyously sharing in Pira's victory,

"...don't worry about your ma. You didn't do anything wrong. Now, come on Young'un, let's clear this mess away. The sun is setting and soon it will be mealtime."

Grandpa's arm around her shoulder turned her away from Pira's happy family. He smiled but it didn't quite meet his eyes, and handed her a piece of flat bone,

"Here you go," he said, before bending to pick up the now scarred and damaged hides from the floor. He folded them carefully and set them to one side. Osha sighed, took the bone and began using it to clean away the small shards littering the floor while larger ones she placed back on the flint pile to be worked.

The sun was close to setting and pink and purple ribbons were strewn across the sky as the day made way for dusk. A cool evening breeze blew around and every so often, Osha found herself having to stop, move away and cough to avoid the swirling dust which threatened to choke and blind her.

"I think that's it for me." Grandpa groaned, holding his lower back and placing his bone tool to one side, "There's not much more to do, just take care with that dust. Come and join us once you've finished, Young'un." He placed a gentle hand on Osha's bent head and walked back towards the family hearth where Osha could see the household gathering ready for the evening.

She couldn't see her brother, but that was no surprise, Polto had friends in other households and often shared meals elsewhere, before returning (noisily) late at night.

Uncle Usso was busy piling the hearth with fresh wood, ready for the meal as Ma and Aunt Cosa sat together while the two smallest children made mischief, as usual.

She sighed and continued with her task until the coughing began to overwhelm her.

Through blurry and sore eyes, she thought she saw something move. A vague outline stood among the tall trees. She wasn't entirely sure, but she could have sworn it was Inko. Blinking rapidly, she used the sleeve of her tunic to gently wipe away the dust. Once her vision cleared, she looked again towards the silhouetted trees, which cast their lengthening shadows over the edge of the camp, but whatever had been there was gone.

Why would Inko be down here at this time of night? she pondered as she placed the bone to one side and surveyed the area. *Maybe it wasn't him.* She didn't have time to speculate further,

"Ohwooooh!" the call echoed around the camp and Osha's stomach growled in response. Leaving all thought of Inko behind her, she scrambled towards the hearth, to be late was to miss out!

Chapter Five

The long summer days continued to pass much like they always had. Osha and Pira helped with small and simple jobs, while also continuing to practise their knapping skills and playing with their younger siblings.

Osha was careful to make sure she obeyed Ma and didn't go back to the cave or mention the strange man in her dreams, who had become a regular presence. There was a sense of calm and harmony about the camp which hadn't been felt in some time.

Winter was approaching: leaves turned gold, then red, then brown and the fruit bushes were picked clean by small animals preparing for their own winters. Polto and Uncle Usso were seen less and less around the camp as they and the other men of the band, began to gather supplies for their annual move south. The weather was rapidly cooling and increasingly, the household snuggled together in their tents under thick reindeer blankets, to stay warm.

"Right, Osha. You and Pira can carry these." Ma barked, frowning at her daughter's face as, grimacing, Osha gingerly took the edge of the heavy reeking skin,

"Hold it carefully, we don't want holes!" Pira's face was as disgruntled as her own as her ma laughed at her,

"Come on Pira, we'll get them nice and clean and then you can help me make some good thick leggings and tunics."

All four had their tunic sleeves rolled up and their hair was tied back away from their faces. This was an unpleasant chore and one that neither girl enjoyed. The mingled stench of animal poo and sweat greeted their nostrils.

"Urgh! This is too heavy, and it stinks!" Osha complained, sticking out her tongue and screwing up her face. Her exaggerated disgust almost causing her to drop the hide.

Ma was not impressed with the dramatics, "Stop it Osha! That's why we're washing it. Keep it above the ground." she snapped, as the bottom of the skin skated the edge of a sharp rock.

"Cosa and I have one much larger and heavier and you don't see us moaning!" she rolled her eyes and pursed her lips. Osha decided it was best to keep quiet.

On reaching the water's edge, they knelt on the bank and gently sunk the hides into the river. Osha could feel the cold and wet of the mud seeping into her thin leggings. She glanced at Pira beside her, catching her eye, and the two girls giggled as they mirrored expressions of disgust.

Ma, however, was far from amused, "Now girls, we need to clean the hides. Stop giggling. Take your stone and rub it over the fur." She instructed. She handed them each a large coarse stone and then looked at them both, her hands on her hips and her face drawn in sharp lines,

"There are only a few weeks until we need to be ready to head south to the winter shelter. If we aren't ready, we will have no effective shelter or winter clothes and stinky hides will be the least of your problems!" The girls looked down at the task at hand, they knew how important preparing the hides was.

Satisfied that they understood the importance, Ma continued, "Use the stones thoroughly, girls, I'd rather not have to wash them again after."

All four set to cleaning their hides. The crystal-clear river slowly grew murkier as they used the water and the weight of their stones to remove the dirt and debris from the thick fur. The water was much colder now that winter was on its way and the rocks were awkward shapes in the girls' small hands. Neither of them enjoyed the dull and repetitive task of working the stone across the filthy hide.

As she worked Osha returned to a familiar daydream; Osha the Fearless. The mammoth rider who crossed lands far away and snuggled at night up against her large hairy friend, she didn't need to clean hides.

It felt like they had been down by the river all day, the water was a disgusting black colour and their hands were sore and turning the colour of the sky on a clear sun-season day. Ma looked over at their hide,

"A good job girls, well done. We can pull them up onto the bank now, after a short rest." she declared.

All four straightened their backs and put their hands under their armpits, a bit of colour returning to them. The two women pulled the girls in for close hugs and together

73

they were cocooned in hide cloaks. The two girls giggled as they felt their bodies warming up,

"Right, that's much better" Ma declared, letting go of Osha and taking her hands in hers. "Time to get these hides on the bank." She blew on the cold fingers and Osha felt the warmth of her breath.

Together, they dragged the waterlogged but now clean hides out of the river. It was hard work as the skins resisted in the strong current. After a few minutes of pulling and careful manoeuvring, the two reindeer hides lay on the grassy bank ready to dry in the sun.

Ma turned to the girls and smiled, the hard lines of her face softening slightly,

"Excellent. I think we may actually have enough for our winter now." She looked at Aunt Cosa "We'll start removing the hair from these later, once they're dry."

"Yes," Aunt Cosa responded nodding, before placing soft arms around Pira and Osha's shoulders and looking at the older woman,

"I think the girls have done such a good job, they deserve a break, Mara." she said, hugging them to her. Ma looked between the two girls, who were displaying the most sweet and innocent smiles,

"You go and have the rest of the day, girls. Take care and don't get into any trouble." she sighed, turning to look at the drying hides. Aunt Cosa winked and gently kissed the top of Pira's head,

"Off you go." The girls didn't need any further encouragement, they held hands and ran off towards the woods, "See you at mealtime!" she called after them.

It had been a good few weeks since Osha and Pira had last had time to themselves, "We're finally free!" Osha grinned, jumping around as Pira laughed and joined in her excitement.

"What shall we do now?" she asked. Osha stopped jumping and thought about all the things they could do.

"How about we play Hunter?" Osha suggested and Pira enthusiastically nodded in response.

This was a favourite of the girls. The aim was quite simply to play the role of predator and prey. Sometimes they would play as animals imitating their calls and behaviour. Other times they would just run around and hide from each other. The trick was to convince the other player that you weren't where they thought you were. Pira had learned an excellent skill from her pa and after a short time of Osha playing as a wolf chasing a bird, Pira's whistle sent her racing off towards the camp. The season-trapped trees of the forest cloaked and distorted the sound and a squawk of triumphant laughter made her realise her mistake.

Loping back through the trees, she saw Pira flapping her wings and hopping on tip-toes as beneath their feet, crunched and squelched layers of leaves and discarded berries.

"I can see you, silly bird" she growled and quickened her pace a little before breaking into a full gallop. Pira's squawked, yelp was muffled as she pounced upon her cousin and the two tumbled to the ground.

Osha shouted in triumph, "Hah! Caught you!" and laughing together, the girls rolled onto their backs and lay looking up towards the canopy of branches that, only weeks before, had been adorned with luscious foliage.

"You wouldn't have seen me if I hadn't laughed!" giggled Pira. Osha nodded,
"Your whistle has got really good. I wish my pa had taught me that..." she stopped realising, of course, the impossibility of that idea.

Pira turned to face her and gently reached for her hand, before looking back into the branches above, "I wish we didn't have to leave here. It's so pretty," she said with a deep sigh. Osha looked at her and smiled before frowning,

"I know. There's nowhere like this down south and..." She stopped, sitting up and looking towards her favourite place in the whole world whispering, "...there's no mammoths."

They had spent several very happy seasons in the northern camp, enjoying the freedom of the local area and admiring the beauty of its landscape which changed as the season progressed. Grandpa ensured they had plenty of fish while the other men focused on the hunting of large and small animals. The range of food they could find was vast and they were all well fed. Then, as winter skulked behind cold winds and bitter nights, they were thrown into concentrated preparation for their journey south, in a moon-cycle or so, where successful hunts were rare and foraging in freezing temperatures could be fatal. As they grew older, this inevitable departure became harder.

Slowly an idea began to form in Osha's head and a devious grin spread across her face. Jumping to her feet, she held out her hand for Pira and helped her up off the cold ground. Her cousin looked at her warily.

"Come on, Pira. Let's go to the cave again. It's been weeks!" Osha said, and her smile grew even wider as the girl reluctantly nodded in agreement.

They brushed the leaves and mud off their tunics and leggings, ensured their shoes were securely on their feet and ran towards the cave together.

Chapter Six

Laughter and heavy footsteps echoed through the dense cloak of trees, as the two young girls raced towards the cave. Stopping as they reached the entrance, Osha turned to Pira and grinned, her face glowing with excitement.

"We're going to see the mammoths!" It had been a long while since Pira had ventured inside the dark cave and she looked at her older cousin, her mouth twisting as she decided how best to respond. Before she could, however, Osha grabbed her hand and pulled her towards a clump of trees, gesturing her to help,

"We need some tree sap and a green stick," she paused and looked around the area. The cave took up most of the ground nearby. Slightly further out were the trees, now barren of life, which she had indicated to Pira as their target. They didn't look promising for finding new growth. She frowned as she thought about the possibilities.

Suddenly, she remembered that as part of the preparation for winter, Grandpa had recently ordered a bunch of branches to be fire-hardened for emergency torches. Her head shot up and she looked at Pira, grinning,

"We need to get some of the branches from the camp." Before the younger girl could object or make an alternative suggestion, she'd raced off. Reluctantly, Pira followed,

"Slow Down, Osha. I can't catch up!" she desperately called after her cousin's receding figure.

Both girls were out of breath by the time they reached the bustling camp. Osha had never seen it so busy. Men she didn't recognise were helping her uncle, moving about all over the camp with bones, hides and weapons gathered in their hands. Grandpa had appeared and was directing this all from the family hearth. The winter preparations were in full swing.

"Where have you two been?" Grandpa smiled at them as he beckoned them over to him. Impatient but recognising she needed to reply, Osha wandered over.

"Helping Ma. We're free now so we're gonna go look at the mammoths, Grampa. I want to remember them while we're away down south." The old man smiled and nodded.

"Well, make sure you come back before sun down." he gestured to the busy camp, "we've got a lot of help at the moment, but could always do with some extra hands once you're done." Osha nodded then remembered why they had returned to the camp in the first place,

"Grampa, it's very dark in the cave. Can Pira and I have a torch, so we can see inside?" In reply, the old man walked over to one of the nearby tents where a pile of branches with blackened ends had been placed and picked up two that were sturdy, but not too long. He handed one to Osha and the other to Pira,

"There won't be enough light using just the torches. Make sure you use these to light the lamps that are in the cave."

Osha wrinkled her nose at the mention of the lamps and Grandpa laughed, "Well if you're going to see the pictures, you'll have to put up with the smell, Young'un." His face turned serious,

"Now, remember. No further than the mammoth cave and be back by sun-down." He said, pointing a crooked finger first towards Osha and then Pira. As they nodded in agreement, he took a shorter stick, pushed it deep within the gently smouldering hearth and with a flickering flame, ignited the ends of their torches.

"There you go girls. Stay safe." He said, turning his attention back to the activity in the camp.

Returning to the cave with their flaming prizes in hand, Osha was struck by how isolated it was. Although you could just about see the tops of the tents in the nearby camp, no sound could be heard from the busy members of the household. Entering the cave itself was as if a wall of silence had cut them off from the outside world.

With the torches casting light ahead of them, ready to ignite the small conifer wicks of each lamp in turn, the two girls steeled themselves for the journey ahead.

"Do you remember the first time we came here, Pira?" she asked, turning towards her. Pira nodded and smiled,

"Yeah. Grampa brought us. It was about two winters ago, wasn't it?" Osha grinned,

"Do you remember what he said about the lamps?" Pira giggled as Osha pulled herself up straight and pointed her finger at her in an impression of their grandpa, "Now, this stuff is made from animal fat, young'uns so it will smell a bit!" She held the torch out towards the first set of lights and they watched in fascination as the yellow flame caught on the small dry conifer branch nestled among the gelatinous animal fat.

The girls laughed at the stench which emanated from the lamp as the heat began to melt the thick fat, but this swiftly changed to coughing as they tried to clear the acrid taste at the back of their throats.

"They're...a...good...light...in...the...caves, if...only...we...could...do...aw...ay...with the...smell!" Pira said trying to imitate Grandpa again as she coughed and wiped her eyes with the back of her hand. The smoke and smell combined to make her eyes sting and water.

"Urgh...He really wasn't wrong...was he? It stinks worse...than...the...hides!" The young girl exclaimed. Osha could barely respond as her own eyes reacted in a similar way while the memory made her laugh.

Turning her attention away from the lamps, she extinguished the flame on her torch, placing it in the belt around her waist and turned to look at the various paintings covering the walls. Osha was eager to take them all in.

Moving from one to another she traced the lines, storing away the feel of every picture, to keep a cherished and nourishing reminder of the beloved cave.

She thought about how different things had been two winters before. Ma had been less angry and had smiled, hugged and danced with her. She turned to Pira,

"Remember after Grampa brought us here, we went back to the camp after sun down and met Korto. He was so small and wriggly." Pira nodded, "Then Lota came not long after. They were like two wriggly slugs!" The two girls giggled, wiggling from side-to-side.

Osha's eye was caught by a particular favourite painting of a rhino. She traced the dark lines that were his horn and reflected to herself that it was after Korto appeared that Ma got angry more. An image of her Ma dancing with a man

86

with pale eyes and laughing, came into her mind. He wasn't the same man in her dreams and he hadn't been there after the cave, but it was good to remember Ma laughing, she really didn't do that much anymore.

She sighed and turned to look at Pira who was looking at a cave lion, "They're so scary looking, Osha" She said as she came up to her. "Big, scary and Grampa said they used to live in these caves!" she turned an anxious face towards her. Osha shook her head a placed a reassuring arm around her shoulder.

"Yeah. But they don't anymore. It's ok. Come on we have a bit further to go to reach Grampa's mammoth, do you remember where it is?" Pira nodded and they continued down the path, holding the lamps as far away from their noses as possible.

"Look at this one." Pira said stopping in front of a lion-like sabre toothed cat, "Isn't it strange Osha. Grampa said they used to hunt around here. Now they're gone." she said, recalling a favourite story of Grandpa's where he'd alone fought off three at once, saving a group of children.

"I dunno, Pira." Osha replied, before pointing at the picture, "Look at those teeth, though!" she said tracing the two long lines descending from the cat's mouth. They giggled together as Osha did an awful fearsome cat impression, but were left pondering that, like the mammoths, these large beasts no longer roamed the wilderness.

The already chilly air grew colder and damper as the two girls moved further into the cave network. As they went, they carefully used previous lamps to light the next ones. There were fewer to be lit here and the uneven ground meant they had to steady themselves against the wall. As they leaned into the clay to maintain their balance, their fingers left gentle impressions, recording their presence.

A short while later, they arrived at the vast cavern in which Grandpa had drawn his mammoth those many winters ago.

When the three of them had first come to this cavern, two winters back, she had been far from impressed. The walls were mostly bare, and the stone was crumbling in many places. She'd longed to be back at the camp, warmed by the fire rather than standing in a cold damp cave. It had only been when the quiet voice of Grandpa had whispered,

"Look up, young'uns." that she'd realised why they'd come this far: the entire roof of the cavern was covered in amazing black paintings of animals. There was a huge elk with its majestic antlers, a rabbit bounding across the grey expanse.

But it was one particular painting which held her attention.

"Can you see it Pira?" she whispered, a thrill running through her as she saw her mammoth again. Her cousin nodded and smiled, pointing at the beloved image just out of reach on the back wall.

Their footsteps echoed around them as they ran towards it, lifting their lamps high. This painting was special. Not just because of its beauty and attention to detail but because this was Grandpa's painting.

As she and Pira stared at the image, she could imagine him as a young man, balanced on poles, their imprints still in the ground, recording the image of the animal with a carefully cut reed and a small bowl of charcoal and water.

Their lamps flickered as a cool breeze blew around the cave. Pira snuggled up to her cousin as a shiver ran through her. Suddenly, she snapped her head up, her eyes fearful,

"Osha. I hear something." She whispered, barely audibly.

Chapter Seven

Osha cocked her head to one side, listening carefully. The cave did strange things to sound. Sometimes in the distance the quiet gurgle of the underground stream could be heard and every so often birds or other animals became trapped in the network so that fluttering wings or skittering feet sounded like spirits howling or scratching at walls.

These noises were also so distorted that you never knew if what you were hearing was coming from outside the cave or further in the network.

This was different though. It was hard to tell what was making it, but the sound was almost like an odd shouting, even barking. Whatever was making it sounded like they might be in trouble. The only problem was, the direction of it came from further into the cave, where they had been explicitly told they were not allowed to go.

Curiosity fought with her sense of obedience to Grandpa as Osha turned towards the sound, "I think we should investigate, Pira. It could be something important. If we're careful and quiet, we can find out if there's any danger to the camp!" she looked at her cousin, whose face showed her worry and concern,

"What if it's a lion or a bear?" Pira asked, knowing that this was likely to make no difference to the headstrong Osha. When it came to the opportunity for adventure, Osha tended to allow her curiosity to draw her in.

"If it's a lion or a bear, we will very carefully and quietly leave to tell everyone about it. Then your pa can sort out a hunting party to deal with it," As expected, Osha's response demonstrated that her excitement had once again overcome her own sense of safety,

"Come on! I'll look after you. Nothing will happen, I promise." she said. As per usual in these situations, Pira reluctantly nodded and followed her cousin as they crossed a line neither of them had before.

Osha had a good idea where they needed to head. Beyond the room they were in, the cave network split into several different pathways. Some lead back to the entrance but the path they needed lead further in. If Pira thought the woods were scary, then this passageway was mind-numbingly terrifying – it was as if the dark swallowed up even the smallest amount of light.

The imaginations of the girls ran wild. For Osha, it was the perfect place for monsters and spirits to lurk, the darkness cloaking their presence as they ventured on.

"It's this way," Osha beckoned to Pira, who nervously edged towards her. Both girls peered ahead into the gloom. They still held their lamps, but the small light was not enough to see very far along the path. Tiny pinpricks cast a glow just at their feet, which would have to do. Looming walls surrounded them, and Osha felt a prickly sense of panic beginning to rise but desperately pushed it down.

This was important. They had to find out what was in the cave.

The path was mostly straight but very long and the girls walked slowly in order to keep safe. Stones and other debris littered the floor, ready to trap unsuspecting little adventurers. Several times they had to grab onto each other as one or the other nearly toppled over.

As they walked, the strange sound could be heard every so often and they knew they were on the right track. It became louder the further they ventured, and its presence was oddly comforting.

"Oh no!" Pira whispered, suddenly standing still. The sound had stopped. They were plunged into silence.

Even the background noises of the trickling stream were gone. Osha lifted her lamp higher in the air to try to see further ahead. She felt she had to say something to try to break through the oppressive pressure around them,

"I think I can see something up ahead. Look." she said into the darkness. The view before them did look different. Where they had previously been able to make out edges of walls, debris littering the floor and the continuation of the path, there loomed a thick blanket of darkness.

Temporarily distracted from her terror at the silence, Pira looked around her, "Hey! There's another lamp here." she called from the wall.

A fizzing sound as the fresh conifer took light, indicated that she'd switched lamps and the dim light was replaced by a brighter flame. Stark realisation made her call out as the fresh light illuminated the scene in front of them,

"Osha. It's the end of the path." She whispered in horror. The path did indeed come to an abrupt end and the strange dark spot was actually a sheer drop to another level of the cave.

Never one to give up, even when faced with a seemingly impossible task, Osha sat down on the edge of the cliff in front of them and considered their options. They could carry on, somehow scale the wall, find the thing making the noise and return to the camp having saved the day or they could return now, never knowing what it was and potentially putting the whole household or even the whole band in danger! Osha knew for certain the best option: this wasn't just an adventure, but a matter of life or death!

Squinting in the meagre light, she looked down into the inky blackness below. It was almost like looking into nothing. If they were to be heroes, they would have to know how far down they needed to climb. She frowned, thinking.

Pira, meanwhile, stood off to one side, twisting a long strand of hair between her thumb and finger on her left hand, the lamp wobbling slightly as she shifted from one foot to the other. She longed for the warming fire of the camp and the comfort of her sleeping mat.

"Osha," she called over to her cousin, who was deep in thought, "we can't go any further. Maybe…maybe we should go home."

The adventurer turned to look at her, her disappointment written in harsh lines across her face. "If you want to go, I'm not going to stop you, but I'm carrying on! We must make sure the band is safe, Pira. No one else knows. This is up to us!" The comforting image of the warm fire disappeared from Pira's imagination, as she knew that she couldn't leave Osha alone. If something were to happen to her deep in the caves, she'd never forgive herself. She sighed and shook her head, admitting defeat once again,

"No, it's ok. I'll stay." She conceded. Osha's frowning face lit up in a grin of triumph,

"Great! Now pass me some of those rocks over there." She replied, pointing to a small pile of rubble which had crumbled from the wall. The younger girl was confused by the request but bent down to pick up a handful of rocks which lay near to where she stood. They ranged in size and almost dropped out of her small hand as she handed them over.

Once again, Osha grinned at her, then took three rocks about the size of horse chestnuts and dropped them one after another into the blackness of the abyss. As she did this, she placed a finger to her lips and turned her head to listen carefully. It did not take long for both girls to hear three clear and consecutive tapping sounds of the small rocks hitting the ground beneath.

"So there is a bottom!" Osha's emerald eyes shone in the light of her lamp, "and I don't think it's much further down to climb than the old oak tree in the woods!" she exclaimed, her voice rising.

The next job was for her to examine how they were going to climb down.

Looking down, she noticed that some parts of the rocky wall were worn down slightly, like they had been used before. The first ones were just below her dangling feet. The surface of these parts was not as smooth and while she investigated with her feet, she found them to be solid.

"Ok Pira, we're going to have to climb down." She knew the younger girl would not react positively to this plan, but it was the only way for them to continue their journey. She beckoned her to come closer, "You see that rock just below us, that's where I'm going to start. Don't worry. I'm going to go first." She said, smiling reassuringly at the younger girl who was shaking her head,

"You can't! What if you fall? You could really hurt yourself!" Pira said, tears beginning to well in her eyes.

"I'm not going to hurt myself silly. I'm going to be really careful. We've climbed up and down further before, I'll be fine! Now watch."

She turned around, gripped the edge, took a deep breath and stretched out to reach the slightly worn stone beneath her. With her other foot, she found another one just beneath. Very carefully she moved her hands one at a time to grip the jutting stones visible just underneath the ledge.

She avoided looking down into the darkness, knowing that if she did she'd panic. It was, indeed, just like climbing down a tree. Except she was in the dark, without anyone standing beneath to catch her and she couldn't see the ground – no problem at all!

About halfway down, Pira's worried face disappeared from her view and the light from the lamp she held went with her. Regret and a feeling that this might have been a mistake, began to grow in her stomach as she descended into the pitch black.

No point regretting it now. I'm nearly there anyway, she thought to herself, as she pushed the feelings deep down.

Slowly and with a great deal of caution, she continued to make her way down the sheer cliff face, searching and finding one stone to grip after another.

Finally, she reached out carefully with her foot and felt solid ground beneath her. The comforting feel of the solid rock was a huge relief and she stepped down onto the ground.

Her arms ached and the muscles in her legs burned from her treacherous climb, but that fact could not stop a huge triumphant grin from spreading across her face.

Standing back from the wall, she looked up to see dark hair crowning a worried face high above her.

"Pira! I made it!" she called up to her anxious cousin, "I'll talk you through your climb down. Do what I did, look for the bits sticking out from the wall." She paused to remove her stick from her belt, "wait a minute, I'll light my torch, so you can see."

Turning away from the wall, she took out a piece of flint and some torn tunic from the pouch on her belt. Striking the flint against the hard ground, she held the material close until the spark caught and lit the end of the torch. Once the flame cast enough light, she called out for Pira to begin her descent.

The light was not significant, but she hoped it would make the climb easier.

Osha watched as the younger girl gingerly turned around and began her own slow descent. From time to time she called out instructions, "Just there, near your hand..." and "Careful, move your feet slightly..." to help with the dangerous climb. Slowly but surely, she watched her make her way down the wall.

"You're doing great, Pira. Almost there!" she called up in encouragement.

The young girl was just above Osha's head, so close to the bottom, when a loud wordless shout echoed from deeper in the cave network.

Osha jumped in fright and looked away from Pira climbing. It was the same sound as before, but this time a lot closer.

Startled, Pira's hand jerked as she reached out to hold onto a nearby stone and the sudden movement caused her to lose her balance.

Osha turned back at the sound of her cousin's anguished yelp as she fell towards the ground beneath.

"PIRA!" Osha screamed as the girl landed on the cold cave floor. Tears streaming down her face, Pira clutched a very twisted and rapidly swelling ankle. Osha raced towards her injured cousin and knelt beside her,

"Ow. It really hurts….it really...really...hurts." Pira whispered in pain.

"It's ok. It's ok. You'll be ok." The now desperate Osha tried to comfort her. It began to dawn on her that nobody knew they were there, so deep in the cave. She gently cradled her best friend in her arms as she tried to ignore this terrifying fact.

What if we're never found? What if whatever had made that strange noise IS a lion or bear and was hungry? She thought, squeezing her eyes together to try to stop the tears from falling. *I must not cry…I…must…not…cry.* Big fat tears rolled down her face, betraying her.

"Don't cry Osha," Pira sniffed as she tried to stop her own tears. Gingerly she moved away from the bigger girl to inspect her ankle. It was swollen and twisted but she could gently move the other foot. Osha looked towards her as she bravely moved her non-twisted foot.

"At least this one's ok." She said, smiling weakly at Osha through a veil of tears.

It was at this moment, that they heard the noise again. Shouting. Nearby and getting closer. Their smiles turned to stone as they listened again to the strange noise.

"It sounds like a person." Osha whispered, desperate not to give away where they were. Pira nodded in silence. "They might be able to help? I'm going to follow it. I'll be back in a minute."

Without checking to see if Pira was ok with this, Osha stood and walked further into the cave. She could hear slow, shuffling footsteps coming towards her.

"H…Hello? Is…Is anyone there?" Osha called into the silence ahead of her. Carefully holding on to the cave wall, she moved to where the footsteps were coming from. Out of the gloom, a tall, thin figure suddenly appeared. A white face with long dark hair and grey eyes loomed a few steps away, its arms were raised menacingly. Its teeth were bared. It was growling.

Osha took a step back in alarm, her mind immediately jumping to tales of monsters and spirits. She was frozen to the spot.

"Oy! What're you doing?" a voice cut through the darkness of the cave. Osha turned and found herself looking at Inko who walked past her to gently take the arm of the strange figure,

"It's ok Ma. Don't you worry. It's only those girls I was telling you about, not an animal." He guided her the direction she'd come, a calm reassuring hand reaching to stroke gentle circles on her back.

Osha scrubbed at her eyes, taking a deep breath to calm her nerves. "She's your ma?" She called after Inko as she followed him down a long, narrow passageway.

"Yeah." came his gruff response, "And I suppose you've found out my secret. Not part of a band are we!" Osha noticed that around his neck hung two dead rabbits. He'd obviously been out hunting. At his waist, were tied some simple tools, much like her own flint.

"You live here? In the cave?" He nodded at her questions.

"Yeah. We move around a lot though. Came here the start of last season. It's a good place. Now once I know Ma's ok, we'll go help your sister." He said, leading them into a well-lit cave to the left of the passage.

"Cousin. She's my cousin." Osha replied as she looked around the small room that he and his ma called home.

"OK cousin then. She took a nasty fall. You gotta be careful scaling that wall, learned that one myself!" he said, turning away to gently help his ma sit down on a ledge at the back of the cave.

The strange woman hadn't said a word. She sat with her eyes closed, gripping the hands of her son and slowly breathing in and out.

Osha looked around at the life they had built for themselves. The cavern was lit by four or five torches and was about the same size as the one which housed Grandpa's mammoth; much smaller than her family's camp. The unlit hearth was to her left and surrounding a large rock on the right, a curious mixture of crudely carved flints and neater, larger tools lay ready to be used. On the other side of the cave was a small pile of furs.

It was a very simple home and she could see that most things had probably been made by the boy. Looking at him, she noticed small silvery marks criss-crossing the knuckles on his right hand; signs of inexpert flint knapping.

As he placed the rabbits down in front of his ma, who was now a lot calmer, she smiled and opened her eyes, before picking up a simple blade and setting to the task of dealing with their meal. He bent down to her and quietly said something, which Osha couldn't hear. The woman looked up, made a few strange gestures with her hands and pointed at Osha. Inko nodded and then stood up.

"Come on. Let's get your cousin." He beckoned to Osha who followed him the way they'd come.

It didn't take long for them to reach the part of the cave where she had left Pira. Osha saw that Inko had given the younger girl a fur to keep her warm. Pira's face lit up as she saw them,

"Oh good. You're back. I was worried you weren't coming." She said in a small voice.

"Silly. I'd never leave you!" Osha replied, shaking her head and smiling at her cousin. She and Inko moved to stand either side of Pira.

"We're going to help you up, but you're going to have to help too." Inko explained what he needed her to do and between them they managed to get her to her feet.

"Ok. Now me and Osha are going to hold our hands to make a ledge for you to sit on, when you've done that, hold onto our necks with your arms." He said, smiling at the younger girl as they proceeded to carry her towards the makeshift home of he and his ma.

Chapter Eight

It was a surprise to Osha that on their return to the cave, Inko's ma was ready and waiting. She gently picked Pira up from the arms of the children and carried her over to a fur blanket which Osha hadn't previously seen.

She laid her down and proceeded to remove her shoe from her foot. Taking a stick from the nearby hearth, she very gently placed it next to the foot. Osha watched as she then wrapped some flax rope around the ankle and the stick supporting it.

The strange woman smiled at her cousin with a look of sympathy as she very gently corrected the twist, causing the young girl to let out a cry, as the foot was placed in the correct direction.

She then took a strange plant, chewed it and placed the green mess on the swollen ankle.

"What is she doing?" Osha asked in alarm. This was something that she had never seen before.

"It's OK. She used to be a healer." Inko explained. Osha looked curiously at the mysterious boy. She couldn't understand how his ma could have these skills but not be a part of a band. As if reading her thoughts, he turned to her,

"We used to have a band. Ma was the healer, then she had me and all that changed." He stopped, looking over at his ma, before lowering his voice and continuing,

"One day we were walking in the forest, I wasn't old, maybe five winters, when we heard shouts and screams coming from our camp. We got there to see a pack of wolves..." He broke off, "Nobody but us was left. We weren't many anyway. So Ma took me, and we've been moving around ever since. It's hard though 'cause she doesn't really speak much. Not anymore."

"How many winters have you seen, Inko?" she looked sympathetically at the strange boy with the sad tale,

"About..." he held up both hands with fingers outstretched matter-of-factly.

A wordless interjection came from the sleeping mat as Inko's ma motioned to the two children. She pointed at Osha and then Pira, before looking at her son and pointing to herself, then she made another of the strange gestures that Osha didn't recognise.

"She wants you to go get someone to help you." the young boy translated. This hadn't been at all clear to Osha, but it made sense. They had been in the cave for many hours and her family would be wondering where they were.

"I'll go with you. It'll be easier to explain with two." Inko said, as he took an already lit torch from the wall, "Pira will be fine here. Ma'll look after her." The woman in the corner smiled kindly at Pira who smiled back.

Osha nodded and followed the light of the torch.

Osha and Inko made their way back along the dark and winding passageway to where Pira had fallen. It felt strange to Osha to be walking with this boy. He seemed different to the rude and surly one she and Pira had met in the forest all those weeks ago. He seemed taller too.

On reaching the spot where the accident had happened, Osha was surprised to see a flaxen rope hanging against the wall, near to the stones that she had used to climb down.

"Where'd that come from?" she said, pointing to the new addition.

"It's how I get in and out of here. I hold onto the rope and use it to climb the wall. It'd be dangerous otherwise." He replied, as Osha looked sheepishly at the ground. She now realised just how dangerous.

Sure enough, the climb with the rope was a lot easier. They still had to go slowly, but it gave an extra level of security: if at any point they didn't feel safe, it was there to hold onto.

Once both children had managed to scramble up the side of the rock, Osha watched as Inko untied the rope before winding it into a loop and attaching it to his belt. They then began to make their way back through the maze of the cave, by the light of Inko's freshly lit torch.

As they were walking, Osha continued to ask questions about Inko and his life to which his answers were short, where had they come from? "North." was his reply. Why couldn't his ma speak? "Dunno." In the end she concluded he didn't really want to tell her.

The sound of voices reached them before they arrived at the entrance of the cave,

"Osha! Pira! Where are you?" It was Grandpa and he didn't sound happy. Behind him were all the men of the band. Osha shouted back, and a wall of long shadows crept around the corner to meet the two children standing there waiting,

Osha had never seen Grandpa so angry. His face was burning red and his voice was the quietest and sternest it had ever been,

"Where've you been?" he demanded, "and who's this? Where's Pira?"

"This is Inko, Grandpa. Remember, I told you about him?" she said, and her Grandpa slowly nodded, "Pira fell and hurt her ankle. She's in the cave, where Inko's ma is looking after her." At the mention of an accident, Grandpa's face changed from angry to very, very worried. He turned to the men behind him and barked,

"Follow the boy! I'm taking her back to the camp." The men were used to following the orders of the oldest in their band and followed as Inko lead them into the caves. As they disappeared around the corner, Grandpa turned to

Osha, a combination of disappointment, hurt and worry all on his face.

"What happened? I told you to be back before sundown. Everyone was so worried."

As Osha looked up at him, her eyes filled with tears. Slowly she started speaking, the whole tale coming out in one go. As she drew to the end and reached the part with Pira's accident, her voice broke and the tears which had threatened before, began to pour down her cheeks. She couldn't bear to look up, instead she focused on her worn and dirty shoes. The end of her tale was followed by silence.

"Don't you ever do that again." He whispered sternly.

"I'm sorry Grandpa, I didn't think." Osha was truly sorry about what had happened. Grandpa didn't say anything further. He reached out, took her small hand in his and marched her out of the cave, into the star filled night.

As she and Grandpa came back into the camp, Aunt Cosa rushed towards them, closely followed by Uncle Usso.

Silent words were exchanged between the three, and Osha was enveloped in the arms of her aunt, while Grandpa drew his son away.

Hot tears of regret and relief streamed down Osha's face as she thought about what could have happened. Through a veil of tears, she could see Ma, standing off to one side, twisting a piece of hide tightly between her fingers. She saw Uncle Usso walk towards her, before his head bent down to hers.

Osha sniffed hard as she felt the tears dripping down her nose. Aunt Cosa moved her to arm's length and gently wiped away the line of tears with a soft thumb.

"Now, now Osha. Everything is ok. My Pira is safe and will be back soon enough." she calmly whispered. Her pale face and forced smile made Osha feel all the guiltier. She nodded in response and did not protest as she was gently guided towards the sleeping tent, her aunt's arm wrapped tightly around her shoulder.

Her sleeping mat and warm fur blanket were a welcome sight. She snuggled down under the fur and closed her eyes. The final thing she remembered before the mammoth's pulled her into dreams, was the feel of soft lips as they brushed her forehead.

Consequently, she didn't witness the fascinating spectacle of a tall, dark haired stranger carrying the injured Pira into the camp. It was only on waking the next morning that she learned what had happened,

"She wouldn't let them carry me." Pira giggled, gingerly sitting up on her sleeping mat and pulling the furs close around her shoulders to keep out the chill, "She can't speak, Osha but you could tell what she wanted. I've never seen any of them like that. They looked like Korto when your ma tells him no!" she looked over to Osha, who was hugging her knees.

"I'm so sorry Pira. I never meant for you to get hurt." she whispered, holding back the tears. Pira looked at her and gently reassured her that she was ok and Inko's ma had really helped her foot, which remained strapped to the stick. This did little to stop her feeling guilty. She knew she had made several mistakes the previous day and there would be consequences.

It was later in the day that she learned what they would be. Grandpa came over to the tent and called her out. With growing fear, she followed him to the family hearth. Everyone was there, all seated around the slowly burning fire. Her ma, who looked at her daughter with a mixture of sadness and something else, sat to Grandpa's left and her aunt and uncle were to his right. Their faces greeted her with small smiles and nods of encouragement. The children were held in their laps and her brother stood behind her ma, one hand placed on her left shoulder. Grandpa's expression was that of a leader. Gone was the smiling, mischievous, paternal figure that she loved. He sat with his family around him and looked sternly at the little girl.

"Inko has told us what happened yesterday. Of course, he doesn't know what happened before and how you came to even be that far in the cave. I've told you and Pira that you're NOT to go that far into the cave. You're very lucky that it was only Inko and his ma there. Bears have been known to live in there, you know." He paused, waiting for the message to sink in. Tears began to roll down Osha's face as she realised Pira could have been right.

"You've acted without thinking and broken a simple rule and my trust. You've seen eight winters Osha, you should know better. I'm very disappointed in you." Grandpa turned his face away, looked from his daughter to his son and then returned to look at Osha.

"I can't allow you to go off on your own like that. Until you can prove to me that you are can follow the rules, you and Pira won't be leaving the campgrounds without an adult guide. Now, have you anything to say for yourself?" He looked pointedly at her, waiting for a response. By this time, Osha was crying so hard that she could barely speak.

"I'm...I'm...really...really...sorry...Grandpa." she sobbed, tears pouring down her cheeks.

Grandpa looked at her, his expression softening. Getting up from his seat, he moved around the hearth and came to stand beside her.

"I accept your apology, Young'un. You made a mistake, we'll forget it now." He pulled her into his side, cradled her head with his other arm and kissed her hair. "We were so worried about you girls."

The poor girl continued to try to regain her breath, hiccupping quietly to herself. She felt a gentle hand on her shoulder and was surprised to see her ma standing next to them. She waited for shouting and hard tones but instead, Ma pulled her into her arms in a deep and loving hug.

"You made a mistake. It's ok now." She whispered into the top of her head, her voice hoarse and unlike anything Osha had heard before. She hugged herself close to her ma in response. She had made a mistake, but it was not one she would EVER repeat, she promised to herself, the land, the spirits and the sky. Never ever again.

Chapter Nine

The next few weeks passed without much drama. Pira's ankle continued to heal as Inko's ma made regular trips down to the camp. At times, Inko came with her and it had become the custom to offer food and supplies to the mother and son in exchange for their medicinal services.

Inko spent a lot of time with the girls and as they got to know him, they found him to be quite friendly. From a group of two they quickly became one of three.

By necessity, anything they did was either within the tent or just outside. Pira couldn't really move from her sleeping mat and they spent their time helping with simple but boring jobs of mending clothing (which Osha hated) or simple bone work. As part of their punishment, flint lessons were stopped. Consequently, Pira was growing increasingly bored as her foot continued to improve.

"Urgh! I don't want to sit here anymore." she said, throwing down the small shoe she was working on. This had been a repeated phrase for the last few days.

Osha looked up from the simple mending she had been instructed to do. She placed the thin hide and bone needle down next to her and looked at Pira,

"Not really anywhere we can go." she was still required to stay in the campgrounds and although she understood why, she was disappointed not to even be allowed down to the river. After keeping her head down for the first week after Pira's accident, she had asked whether the restrictions might be lifted ever so slightly.

Grandpa's face and stern shake of the head had given her the answer.

Pira sighed and stretched her legs as far as she could on the mat. The swelling in her ankle had almost disappeared and she had been able, with support, to walk a short distance. The concern in the camp was whether she would be able to walk the long distance to their summer camp.

With good conditions, the trip could take about a day. With her inability to walk further than a few metres, however, it would take them much longer to reach their winter home.

At night, when she had been sent to bed, Osha could hear the whisper of conversations as the adults discussed the issues the band faced.

"Hey there." A cheeky face framed with long shaggy hair, appeared around the entrance to the tent. Inko held up a strange looking piece of bone. Holes had been put into it all the way along. Osha looked at the object curiously,

"Hey Inko. What's that?" she asked. He came into the tent and sat down on one of the empty sleep mats. Rather than saying anything, he placed the end of the strange bone in his mouth and blew. To her surprise, a high-pitched sound came out of it.

"What was that?" she said in surprise. Inko grinned and handed it to her.

"You try! Put your fingers over the hole and blow over it." This she did but couldn't make the sound Inko had.

"It's a little tricky," he said, taking the object back. "It's a musical instrument. My uncle used to play it." This was first time he had mentioned any of his lost family. Osha didn't ask anything further, as he placed the instrument to his lips and played a simple but sad sounding tune.

"Can I try?" Pira asked from the corner, her feeling of boredom disappearing in the excitement of something new.

Inko finished his tune and handed the precious pipe to her. Placing it tentatively to her lips, she blew while positioning her fingers over one or two of the holes. Unexpectedly, the instrument made a sound. It wasn't as sweet as Inko's, but with a little more blowing and some guidance, she was able to make two different sounds. She grinned at Osha,

"That was amazing, Pira!" Osha exclaimed. It was good to see the young girl smiling again.

Just then, a shout came from outside the tent. Grandpa was calling the children to the family hearth. Together, they helped Pira to stand and slowly walked towards the sound of voices.

All the main members of the band were gathered around the hearth. Grandpa, as always, was leading and the men and women from the area looked at him with a strong air of respect. He smiled as he stood with Inko's ma on one side. He beckoned Inko to him and addressed the crowd of about thirty people.

"Friends and family, I have gathered you here today for several reasons. The first is to say thank you," he turned to Inko's ma, whose head remained bent in shyness, "without the kindness and support of this woman and her son, we may not have found my two young granddaughters. Her demand to take care of young Pira, has saved her from the arms of the spirits and we are forever grateful." He paused as the crowd cheered and clapped for Inko's ma, who briefly lifted her head and smiled.

"For too long these two, Inko and Ana have had to fend for themselves alone. They have had no comfort of family or support of a band. I have invited Ana and Inko to join us and to gain that support and comfort by becoming a part of our family."

Inko looked at the girls' surprised faces and grinned. Grandpa continued, "Ana has shown me how we can get Pira part of the way to the southern shelter. I need five strong men to help myself and my son, Usso, with this task…"

Osha's attention switched off from the rest of what Grandpa had to say as Inko came over to their side, still grinning,

"So I'm gonna be one of you lot!" Osha had never seen his smile wider. She wondered what life must have been like for him all these winters, caring for his ma; needing to move on as soon as local resources were gone; not having any sense of a home. She was pleased Grandpa had offered them this chance at a new life.

"Yes you are!" she said, clapping him on the back, as a grinning Pira hobbled over to them. Excited about the future, all three returned to the warmth and comfort of the tent. Inko once again picked up his flute and helped Pira play it.

Over the next few days, the activity in the camp, which had been busy before, suddenly intensified. People moved continually through the camp and Osha was required to be helping constantly.

To one end of the campground, Grandpa and the five men busily prepared the special seat for Pira from two vast reindeer antlers, wood and reeds, as Inko's ma, Ana, had suggested. She watched closely as his ma stood near the men, giving directions using her hands and making sounds of irritation every so often.

The seat was very strange looking. Luckily, Pira was not heavy and it was easy to see how it could be used. Ana and Osha's ma spent a lot of time together, working hard to weave a simple mat which would take the girl's weight. Osha didn't know what they talked about or how Inko's ma made herself understood, but whenever she saw Ma, she would pull her daughter into a hug.

When the seat was finished, the men carried it over to the tent, helped Pira to sit on it and took the long rope, showing how the strange contraption could be pulled. They would have to stop every so often, but it was important that Pira spent some time walking as well.

Finally, everything was ready, and it was time to leave the campground. Osha would have loved to have had the opportunity to visit the mammoths for one last time, but Grandpa had made it clear this was part of the punishment. Instead, she had to make do with standing on the edge of the campsite.

The ground was covered in a blanket of yellow and red while the skeletal trees stood as a reminder of the looming winter. Images of the mammoths and all the other creatures filled her head, as she peered in the direction of the dark cave.

Once again, she was the mammoth rider, crushing fallen leaves beneath her feet. She turned as the unsteady crunch of long fallen leaves signalled the arrival of Pira, who limped over to stand beside her, before leaning against one of the trees.

"We'll be back before you know it, Osha. Come on, Grandpa wants us to pick up our packs." she said, placing a comforting hand on the older girl's shoulder.

Osha supported Pira, as the two girls walked to where their sleeping tent had been. It was now packed away and tied with flax strings, ready to be taken south. The tall tent poles still remained as they would until they returned. Moving to a natural shelter meant they had no need for them. Between them all, they would move their entire lives on their backs and in their hands. Osha picked up the small packs that had been neatly left for them.

The sun was low in the sky and up ahead could be seen a bank of cloud, as they all gathered together, ready to leave. Grandpa, warmly wrapped in a magnificent reindeer hide, was up front ready to lead the way.

The hard work in the camp over the last few weeks showed in the warm fur coverings that everyone wore.

Bringing up the rear, were her uncle and aunt, pulling Pira in her strange seat. Inko and his ma, Ana, walked just in front of them. In his hands, he carried his pipe, wrapped tightly in a piece of hide and tied with flax.

Turning around one last time, Osha looked again towards the cave. From where she was standing, she could just about see the run of trees which surrounded the clearing outside the entrance. A maze of branches blocked her full view, but in her mind, she traced the different paths she and Pira had taken throughout the season, as echoes of playful cries and laughter filled her ears.

Letting out a deep sigh, she turned away, pulled the flax strap of her package onto her shoulder and stepped into the wilderness.

Chapter Ten

Hilly terrain and seemingly endless grassland stretched out in front of them. The day was cold and they all pulled their fur coats close around themselves to keep out the growing wind. The sun had long-since disappeared behind a bank of steady growing grey cloud. The worst thing that could happen would be to be faced with rain, which could turn to sleet and snow.

Osha's ears were beginning to redden as the wind picked up. "It's getting colder." she whispered as her eyes looked towards the darkening sky. If it got worse, they'd have to find shelter before even being halfway to their destination.

Grandpa was still marching ahead; leading the way, commanding the band. Behind him the various members of the different households talked, laughed and generally entertained themselves. This migration was an annual event and although it wasn't easy, the families generally looked on it as an opportunity to socialise and engage with people they didn't normally see. Osha loved seeing families greet each other with smiles and cries of "How are you?" and "I haven't seen you in so long!".

There was a genuine feel of love and care for one another. These people had been a part of the same extended family for decades. Like her sister Kita, different people from different households had joined together and the band continued to grow and grow.

Grandpa had predicted that it would take them a full day to reach the shelter. By about halfway, most of the fitter members of the five households had moved ahead. Other than Uncle Usso and Grandpa, it was mostly women and children who were left with the group.

Pira was being pulled along by her parents. The strange seat wasn't very comfortable, despite the carefully woven base and back that Ana and Osha's ma had crafted. As Osha walked beside them, she tried to distract her cousin from the discomfort of her transport.

"You're so lucky being able to sit down most of the way!" she said, hoping the gentle teasing would raise a smile on the sulking girl's face. Unfortunately, Pira was not in the mood and turned a highly unusual scowl towards her cousin.

"Hmph. I'd much rather walk with you!" She said, crossing her arms. Osha didn't really know what to do. It was so rare for Pira to be grumpy (that was usually her own role). Turning to her aunt and uncle, she started to say that maybe they should stop for a bit, when her uncle turned to his partner,

"I think maybe we should take a break. Pira can stretch her legs and walk." He said, smiling at his scowling daughter, "What do you think, Pira?"

She didn't need asking twice. Once her ma and pa had stopped pulling the seat, she gingerly moved off and allowed Osha to help her to her feet.

"Now, be careful Pira. You don't want to be hurting it more." her ma said. Pira nodded as she and Osha moved away from her parents.

Osha was pleased to see her friend smiling again. She watched as her uncle wrapped the pulling ropes up before picking up the strange seat.

Ahead of them were Inko and his ma, who had walked slightly quicker than them. She gently took her cousin's arm as they attempted to catch up to their friend,

"Inko. Inko. Wait up!" Osha called after the figure who was holding onto his ma's thin arm as they walked along.

Hearing her daughter's shout, Osha's ma, who was holding the hands of the two youngest in their household, came up and quietly spoke to Ana. Both women were smiling, and Osha watched her ma hand over her youngest cousin, Lotta to Ana while motioning to Inko to join the girls - she would look after his ma.

As the two women and youngest children moved off, Inko casually leaned against a stout oak tree, waiting for the girls to catch up. Noticing Pira was beginning to struggle with their slightly quicker pace, Osha motioned to him to help her support her cousin.

They were now right at the back of the travelling party. It was strange to watch the distance between different groups increase as movement ebbed and flowed like the tide.

Descending further into the valley, they were careful to keep their footing. The increasingly steep ground was very hard beneath them, due to the rapidly freezing conditions and if they were to fall they could have ended up with more than a broken ankle.

Osha looked again towards the growing bank of clouds that now were not only behind them but also in their path. The temperature had dropped drastically too, and she expected that before long they would be walking in a rainstorm.

"In a few weeks, this'll be covered in snow." She said, turning to Inko. She forgot sometimes that they hadn't long met him and his ma. They had so quickly fallen in with their small household.

Up ahead, Osha noticed that the rest of the band had come to a stop on the flatter ground. A large group of trees stood nearby and as the wind began to pick up, swirling around, Grandpa gathered everyone together.

As they came upon the large group of people, they felt the drops of rain on their heads which signalled the start of a deluge.

"Everyone into the trees!" Grandpa ordered. He knew it was important that they keep as dry as possible. Rain, when cold, would freeze and if they tried to continue walking in bad weather, that could cause many health problems.

Once Grandpa was assured that everyone was beneath the safety of the dense trees, he turned to them all,

"It looks like this rain will be here for the rest of the day, certainly until nightfall. We need to make a temporary camp here among these trees." At his command, the adults in the group split off and began to find some supplies. Grandpa, with the help of others, then set about constructing a small hearth.

For the next few hours, the rain continued, as Grandpa had predicted, and the band sheltered together among the trees. The fire was for warmth more than cooking as each household had ensured they had plenty of dry meat to eat on their journey.

As they gathered together, Grandpa told stories of other times that he had had to shelter from bad weather. These were stories that the girls had heard before and so they sat a little further off quietly talking while taking it in turns to play a tune on Inko's pipe.

"What is the shelter like?" Inko asked, as Pira tried to play a simple ditty. Osha turned to him and smiled.

"It's cut out from a cave. You climb up this really steep hill and there is all these stone walls on top. It's a bit like the mammoth cave but open to the sky. You can stand at the top and look across the river to the trees and it's so pretty." She replied, smiling.

"There's nothing to do though," Pira said, taking a break from playing for a moment. Osha nodded,

"Yeah, it's cold, very cold, so we spend a lot of time like this. Ma gives us small jobs to do like mending and cleaning, but we can't really go anywhere. There's no freedom and definitely no mammoths." Osha sighed.

As they were talking, Ma brought around some of the dried meat which they took and ate while continuing their conversation accompanied by Pira's frustrated attempts on the pipe.

"Where did you live last winter?" Osha asked Inko. She was still curious about his life before she'd met him.

"Here and there," he replied, before going quiet again. Osha guessed that he didn't really want to talk about it, but she was not one to leave alone a topic which interested her. She moved closer to him,

"Was it lonely Inko? With just you and your ma?" The boy turned to her and nodded. He then began to explain a little about his life before he and his ma had come to the cave.

Pira stopped playing as she and Osha listened as the young boy poured out his years of loneliness. Tears pooled in his eyes as he quietly explained how they needed to constantly keep moving as each area they were in ran out of resources.

He could hunt small creatures such as rabbits and he wasn't too bad at fishing but on his own he could never hope to take down a large animal. Taking his ma hunting was out of the question as well, "She hates to be anywhere near animals that could be dangerous. She gets really scared and can't move at all." He looked down, clasping his hands together, "I did my best by her. I tried really hard. But...but..." he paused, took a deep breath and looked at the girls, tears still glistening in his eyes, "sometimes I had to find things from other people."

"What do you mean?" Pira asked, putting her arm around the boy's shoulders.

"I...I...I had to take things...without them knowing. If I hadn't ma might've died." His voice rose a little as he confessed his secret. Osha smiled kindly at him, put her own arm around his shoulders and tried to reassure him,

"Well you won't need to take stuff anymore. If you want anything, you ask. Everyone'll be willing to help. You're part of our band now. One of us!" The young boy smiled at this and nodded.

The evening grew a lot colder and the rain continued unabated. Even if it stopped, they would have to stay among the trees for the night. Grandpa and the rest of the adults set about ensuring there were some form of shelters available. They were loath to unpack too much and searched for the best natural shelters in the area.

Once satisfied with each party's situation, Ma came over and handed rolled woven sleeping mats to the children, encouraging them to lie down under the canopy of a vast oak tree,

"It'll keep you safe from most of the rain." she said, smiling. Osha couldn't help reflecting on the change in her ma since Inko and Ana had arrived, she seemed calmer and happier too.

As Osha's ma moved on to speak to other groups, the children organised where they were going to sleep. The ground was covered in leaves and acorns were scattered all around. Brushing them away, they made space for their mats, lying down under the thick animal skins which had been laid beside them.

Slowly the busy group settled down and quiet descended, as the dead of night fell over the makeshift camp. While Osha and the others slept, a lone figure sat watch by the hearth, a spear at his feet. Pira would not have to worry about lions, wolves or any other danger.

Chapter Eleven

The next morning, the rain had stopped. Overnight there had been a hard frost, as the harshness of winter began to roll across the land. Osha and her friends woke to a glistening canopy as the frosty sun hit the frozen trees. All was still. They huddled together beneath their thick furs.

There was no time for a morning meal. The night had left the ground and air completely frozen and Grandpa was very keen to get moving. He hoped they may reach their destination by sundown, despite their unexpected stop.

Once again, sleep mats, furs and necessities were packed away, and they returned to their trek along the grasslands. All were eager to reach their winter shelter and there wasn't much conversation as everyone focused on staying moving to keep warm.

As the day progressed, the temperature plummeted, and the force of the wind increased. Everyone walked with their heads down and furs wrapped tightly around them against the freezing air. Voices were silent as they focused on walking safely. No longer was the group walking freely, they now huddled as closely together as possible, while still allowing themselves enough room to walk.

Osha and Inko walked beside Pira who no longer complained about being pulled on her strange seat, she was the warmest of all. They were all wrapped inside the thick reindeer hides and Osha and Inko held onto each other to maintain some body heat. Nearby were the rest of their household. Grandpa led but made sure to keep close to the rest of the group.

"It's so cold." Osha shivered. Despite her layers of fur, she could barely feel her fingers or nose. Around her, other faces too showed the effect of the winds.

Osha hoped that it wasn't much further to the shelter. She couldn't remember ever being this cold. Hunger gnawed at her belly too, a familiar but uncomfortable feeling that had not been missed. The biggest difference between these next months and those spent in the open camp was the availability of good food.

The sight of the sparkling river, a few hours later, was a welcome sight. From their position they could see a small glow casting a warm light in the distance up above the valley, which became brighter and warmer as they continued walking. They could feel the change in the air - the location was a natural shelter from the frozen winds, which was why it had been chosen all those years ago.

"Not much further now," Osha whispered to Inko, trying to conserve as much warmth as possible. It was still necessary to keep the furs wrapped around them, but with the winds less biting, they could afford to walk separately.

As a group, they ascended the hill towards the shelter. The sight of those of the band who had gone ahead, ready to take packages and carry little ones, was very welcome.

The group included Osha's brother, Polto, who came down towards them holding out a hand to her and Inko, helping them climb the last few steps.

Before them, towered a vast stone wall, a completely natural shelter created many, many years ago. It formed part of the cliff face which sat above the river, far below. No one knew how it was that this safe shelter had come to be, and no one asked. As Grandpa told it, their ancestors had needed somewhere warm when the winters arrived, and they had found it just when they needed it.

As a part of Grandpa's household, Osha and the others always took the middle level of the shelter - it was the biggest and warmest. There were two other levels that were then shared between the four remaining households. One was close to the water while the other had a spectacular view over the river and into the woods - an ideal lookout.

"Here we are then, Inko. What do you think?" Osha moved to stand beside the already blazing hearth, warming her hands. She'd removed the furs and the heat from the fire was finally allowing her nose to thaw.

"It's amazing!" Inko's eyes widened as he took in the surroundings of the shelter. He moved towards the edge, to look down into the quickly darkening evening and Osha, her hands and face warmed, joined him. They both stared down at the slowly moving river. Grandpa came over and placed an arm around their shoulders.

"Ah. I remember the first time I came here as a boy," he said, a faraway look in his eyes. "It was as cold as today, that I can tell you, colder even! Snow was on the ground right up until we reached the river, then nothing but slightly chilly air. It ain't even that far from the summer camp, but it's so different that our ancestors knew this was the place for them."

He slowly drew the children with him towards the warm fire where Pira and their mas sat. Chatter and laughter filled the air as the whole family began to prepare their first meal in their new but familiar home.

There followed many further days of simple meals. No longer were they able to hunt large animals. Instead, the men ventured just far enough into the woods to snare small creatures. Rabbit was a favourite and the men would go out early to catch as many as they could. Sometimes they would have dried fruit and nuts that had been collected before they left their summer camp. Generally though, food was scarce, and hunger was a constant problem.

The children spent much of their time by the hearth, telling stories and practicing their music. With a lot of help from Inko and Pira, Osha had become much better at playing the pipe and Polto had even begun making one for each of the girls. Their supply of bones was not huge, but it was not necessary to use anything particularly large. It was Inko who drilled the holes in just the right spot and worked the end to have the recognisable shape of the mouthpiece.

Grandpa had been properly teaching the lad about the creation of flints and Inko became a part of the knapping competition, quickly demonstrating a natural flair. Osha was very put-out the first time that he won. The size and quality of the winning piece was amazing.

"I haven't ever done one that big!" she exclaimed, quizzing him to learn how to use the feel and sound of the hammer-knocked flint to accurately split the best flake from the core.

"It's easy!" he proclaimed, once again knapping a brutal looking flake. Due to these successes, Grandpa moved the lessons on to looking at creating serrations in the side. The ring of stone on flint carried across the valley, as they spent their time learning how to pressure flake their flint shards.

Pira was not at all bothered by this venture, the small cuts on her fingers pointed to her difficulty in keeping her hammer straight. After another session of bleeding and pain, she begged Grandpa to let her focus on hide work. With his agreement, she spent the time practicing how to craft shoes rather than weapons.

About four weeks after they had arrived in the winter camp, the children were once again gathered around the hearth. Pira had on her lap the hide to make a pair of shoes and the other two were busy challenging each other to create the best finished blade, hilt and all.

The younger girl carefully held a delicate bone needle between her fingers as she stitched the pieces of hide together. She had become very skilled at threading the thin fibre through the eye of the needle. To begin with, it had taken many attempts and much squinting to be able to complete the difficult task.

"There nearly finished." Osha said, holding up her blade to inspect the serrations she had made along one edge. The leather on her lap was covered in small shards of flint that had been chipped from the edge of the larger shard.

Inko's lap too was covered with the sharp pieces of stone. He held up his blade, looked at it carefully, then returned it to his lap to chip away at a section that wasn't quite right.

Osha watched him as he did this several times. She couldn't see why he needed to, it looked perfectly fine to her. Her quizzical look made him smile, "It's got to be perfect. I want to be the best I can." he said.

"Yeah but how can you tell it's perfect?" she replied, pointing towards his blade.

"Each serration needs to be the same size and length, otherwise it won't cut things evenly," he leaned over to pick up a piece of wood which had fallen from the hearth and used the blade to score a mark, "give yours here and I'll show you," with Osha's blade in hand, he made another mark next to his own, "can you see that the mark I made was much cleaner than the one with your blade. Yours will work, but mine is better."

Osha nodded, it was clear that the mark he had made first was neater and went deeper into the wood.

The sound of the hunting party returning meant that it was time for them to clear away. The success for last few weeks had been sparser than usual, and three was concern about why that may be. Consequently, Grandpa had gone on the hunt earlier that morning, to try and assess the situation.

As he appeared in the cave, he held a single rabbit in one of his hands and in the other was a spear. He smiled at the children, placing the rabbit down on a nearby rock ready for it to be prepared. Walking over to the children, he held out his hand for the two blades, ready to inspect their handiwork.

"These look good. You've managed to make the serrations nice and neat and not too far apart. Good work you two." Osha and Inko grinned at Grandpa and each other at his praise.

"So you can now be tidying away your leathers and shards. Pour them onto the dump outside."

They proceeded to do this and once they had finished, Pira joined them in helping as Ma, Ana and Aunt Cosa returned from visiting other groups. Together they all worked to prepare the rabbit which meant they were able to work very quickly. The three women did the more delicate job of skinning the small animal before handing it to the children to cut up. Osha was very excited to be able to use one of her own scrapers to help remove the meat from the bone. The small shard of flint fit perfectly in her hand and was ideal for the job, shaped just so it would scrape without damaging the delicate meat. It wasn't a particularly large rabbit, but it would be the first meat they had had in days.

Grandpa proceeded to tell them about his day, "Taking advantage of the clearer and calmer weather, we set out early. I and the rest of the hunting party came across a group of rabbits but could not find other animals. In four groups we stalked the different rabbits and managed to come away with six. One of which sits before you. We may have to try and dry some. It'll last longer." He then turned to speak to Osha and Inko, directly,

"Now, you two, Tomorrow I want you to come hunting with me. It's time that you learned how we do this." Grandpa smiled as Osha's face lit up. She had never been allowed to go hunting before.

"Really Grandpa? Really, really?" she said, her eyes widening. Inko was slightly more reserved, after all he had been hunting for a long time, but the opportunity to do so with a band wasn't something he had experienced.

"Can we take our own weapons?" He asked, holding up one of the spears that was lying nearby. It was one he'd made a few days before and was especially proud of. The blade was attached to the long wooden pole with a tight wrapping of reeds. Osha nodded in agreement,

"Yes! Yes please, Grandpa! I want to be able to use my own weapon!" The old man chuckled in response and smiled as he replied,

"Of course you can. There isn't much point you making the things if you aren't gonna use them!" At this, Osha jumped up and ran over to hug him. "And you Pira, are you going to come hunting with us?" he said, peering round at her.

Pira looked at the excitement on Osha's face and shook her head, "No, I'll stay here and work on these boots. I think hunting and knapping is more their thing than mine." she said, holding up the pair she had been working on. Osha's face fell slightly, but she understood. She gladly hung on to the old man's neck and pecked him on the cheek.

"Thank you, Grandpa!" The old man continued to smile as he hugged his grateful granddaughter.

Chapter Twelve

The next day found the three ready to leave the camp, joined by various men and women of the band. The plan was for the children to keep with Grandpa while the other, more experienced hunters worked groups to find larger and possibly harder to kill quarry.

Ma and Ana were stood to one side, ready to see them off. Ma held a piece of hide in her hand and was twisting it back a forth as Ana had her arm linked tightly through hers. Osha smiled at her reassuringly, she didn't know why she looked so worried.

"Now Osha, can you remember that rule that I've told you about many times before?" Grandpa said, drawing her attention back onto the excitement of the day. Osha turned to look at him and thought very hard back to the conversations she had had with Grandpa. She knew it was something he talked about often but couldn't quite remember,

"Patience!" the word came to her just as the older man had started miming it.

"Absolutely, my girl! Patience, yes! Today you're gonna must be very patient. Now I need to check that we have all our supplies before heading off." He motioned to the pack that they each carried. The previous night he had spent a good hour instructing them what a good hunter always had with them. Osha proceeded to reel off the list back to him,

"I've got my dried meat, spare blades, my knife, some fruit, some hand axes and a spare animal skin. I've also got my water skin and am wearing well-stuffed boots." This last she indicated by pointing at her feet where her legs were hidden among clumps of grasses. Pira had helped to stuff their shoes the previous evening. They had both joked that the amount of grass in one pair would probably have been enough for both, but Pira had insisted (rather forcefully) that they had to make sure they were warm. In her view it was better to have sweaty, smelly feet than your toes falling off from being frozen. Neither of them could really argue with the logic.

Grandpa appeared satisfied with the preparedness of his young hunters and nodded at them both, "Excellent. It looks like we are ready to head off. It's gonna be a long day, young'uns, so make sure you take care with them boots. Don't want your feet freezing." He grinned. He too had been there when Pira was on her grass rampage and had witnessed the stuffing of the shoes to the point that they could barely move their feet.

All three waved to Ana and Osha's ma as they prepared to set off.

The ground was cold but not icy. The sun held little warmth and a cold breeze swirled through the trees. Osha was very glad that she not only had her spare fur in her pack, but also was wearing one of the thick reindeer hides that had served her so well on the journey down to the camp. It would hopefully warm up as the day progressed and the lazy sun reached further into the sky. If the spirits were on their side. If not, it would continue to be a very cold day.

They were, at this point, walking among the trees near to the river. Grandpa had suggested that they first try to see if they could find anything near the area of their success the previous day. It was deep in the woods, protected from the worst of the weather and a likely spot for rabbits and other small mammals to hide from the cold.

"OK young'uns, we're gonna wait here. We need to hunker down and be ready to go when I say." He pointed to a clearing just ahead where dormant brambles provided some shelter.

"See the small brown pellets on the ground?" the two children looked to where he pointed and nodded, "know what they are?"

Inko immediately responded, "Rabbit poo. You can use it for tracking where rabbits are."

"Ay. Well done Inko. You caught a rabbit before?" the young boy nodded

"Well you can have a go if we see one. But first we must wait. Patience, remember?" Osha grinned and nodded as Inko checked the sharpness of his spear by drawing it across the nearby tree trunk. Grandpa handed them a bunch of pine needles and they rubbed the smell of pine all over their clothing. Satisfied that they were ready, Inko bent his knees so that he was still on his feet but much lower;

hunkered down as Grandpa had called it. Osha copied the movement and Grandpa stood behind, watching the clearing very closely.

The pine trees in front of them gave very good cover and they made sure the wind was blowing away from them, to mask their scent.

The sun moved across the sky and, luckily, the air began to become a little warmer. The temperature rose from below zero, to just about zero and the children were relieved Pira had been so insistent on their grass filled boots. Still they waited for any sign of the rabbits who had left behind the small piles of evidence.

Osha could feel the muscles in her legs beginning to ache. Gently lowering her knees to the ground helped to ease the strain. It was very strange staying in the same position for so long as well as not speaking. She couldn't understand how Inko looked so unconcerned. He was hunkered down ready to go if need be. His face was calm. He had his spear in hand. He looked like an eagle, ready to swoop down onto his prey whenever it appeared.

She glanced at Grandpa. He too looked frozen in time, the cold having stopped his movement completely.

Suddenly a flash of grey caught their six eyes and they turned to watch as several small animals made their way into the clearing. Inko placed his spear down and slowly, so as not to startle them, moved forward step-by-step.

Osha watched as he moved closer and closer to his target. She noticed that he held a small piece of hide with strings attached to it in one hand, and in the other a small piece of flint. He folded the piece of hide and placed the flint inside. Next with his arm extended, he swung the hide, by the strings, above his head.

Osha watched him let go of one string, the flint sailing out of the hide, before it hit one of the animals in the head.

The rabbit immediately slumped forward, and the others scattered. Slowly, Inko moved towards it. Bending over the knocked-out creature, he motioned to Osha who crept over to him, relieved to finally be able to move. He mimed using the spear to finally kill the animal and Osha did so.

Grinning, they returned to Grandpa who smiled at their success.

"Congratulations! Your first successful hunt, excellent teamwork too. Rabbit stew again for our meal it looks like." The two children grinned at him. "Right put it down here and we can go see if we can find any more."

They placed the dead rabbit down on the hide which Grandpa had brought with him to carry their haul back to camp.

Further exploration led them to several similar clearings. Osha made sure to keep her eyes open for evidence of anymore small creatures but saw none. Still, they enjoyed the day and they avoided getting cold, wrapped up in hides with warm, if a little sweaty, feet. Grandpa took the opportunity to point out certain spots and naturally occurring advantages that they could take when on a hunt. Finding cover and tracking the movements of animals seemed to be the most important lessons that he felt the need to impart and Osha was reminded of the game she and Pira played.

The children were given a full list of things to think about when launching a hunt as well as tips for surviving in the world outside of the shelter and protection of the band: finding water, building shelters and the like. It was never too early to learn these skills, was his motto.

As the sun began its descent, the warmth quickly began to disappear, and they were grateful for bringing extra hides to pull on. Osha sighed in relief as her cold shoulders and arms began to heat up.

It was strange being in the centre of the forest. She had no idea how far away they were from the shelter, it could be minutes away or hours.

She was disappointed to have only had one opportunity to practise her hunting skills but had enjoyed the day with Grandpa and Inko. They may not have talked much, but just taking part in an activity she hadn't been able to before, was a refreshing change. She smiled at Grandpa, pleased that he had given her this opportunity.

"I think we might need to call it a day. Much better to return and get warm by the fire. That's another important lesson, young'uns: don't overstretch yourself." he said.

The children definitely weren't going to disagree with this idea. The image of a warm hearth and some of Ma's broth, sent a shiver up Osha's spine. They gathered their things together (although there wasn't much) and prepared to return to the safety of the shelter.

"I wish we'd got something else. Hoped I might've got a deer." Inko's face showed some disappointment that he hadn't.

"Well Young'un. Deer are more a summer hunt. Might've got a boar, but again, they're likely further south." Grandpa put his arm around the boy to comfort him. "When we return to the summer camp, I'll help you catch a deer." Inko smiled up at his adopted grandpa.

"Can I get a deer too, Grandpa?" Osha responded.

"Aye, my girl. We'll go hunting for a small deer together." With that both children were satisfied, and they proceeded to return the way they had come.

They didn't have to walk far before they came upon other members of the band. Several were carrying a decent sized wild boar. Polto came up to them and pointed at the beast.

"I got that one!" He grinned from ear to ear as Grandpa slapped him on the back in congratulations and the young man re-joined the group as they made their way back.

Osha noticed that the group wasn't quite as big as when they had first left that morning. She puzzled over this for a little while but as she was growing tired, she didn't worry about it for too long.

The forest seemed to stretch on for miles ahead. She didn't really think so much about the broth anymore. It was the idea of her soft and warm sleeping mat that drew her home. It was definitely cold now. The hide was keeping most of it out, but every now and then a chilled wind exposed a vulnerable piece of skin and she had to adjust the fit of it.

She knew better than to ask how much further they had to go, but she was definitely questioning her earlier assertion that they weren't hours away from camp. It was becoming harder and harder to put one leg in front of the other.

"Oy! Oy there!" The sound of shouting voices piqued her interest and she wasn't the only one of the group. Grandpa stopped, motioned for the others to also and moved towards the sound.

"Ay! Who goes there? What is the problem?" The commanding bellow of the band leader called to two men whom Osha recognised as some of those she'd noticed were missing but she was not able to name them.

As they came closer, flushed faces and heavy breathing indicated they had been running. Running hard. As they tried to catch their breaths, Grandpa caught up with them.

"What is it lads? You look like you've seen a spirit!" his voice betrayed his concern.

"Not...a...spirit, Anso...a...a..." one stopped and took another deep breath before whispering a word which immediately sapped all the tiredness out of Osha and renewed her like a baby bird after a feeding.

"...Mammoths!"

Chapter Thirteen

"Mammoths?!" Grandpa was incredulous.

"Aye. Back there, on the grassland. Three of them. Two big ones and one little." the man whom Grandpa had spoken to had recovered his breath. He looked down as a small girl with dark burning hair came up to him and tugged on his tunic.

"Would you take me to see the mammoths? I've never seen one." a small voice came from her, wide green eyes open in amazement at the prospect of fulfilling her dream. The man looked quizzically at Grandpa, who nodded, smiling.

"Aye Young'un. I'm not gonna stop you seeing one of the most majestic creatures on this Earth. My, we have the spirits' blessings to be given this opportunity. They must not be harmed. My, I haven't seen a mammoth in…" he paused as he counted out the time in his head, "…must be twenty winters at least!" he turned to the two men. "Now you've seen them, so I need one of you to go back to the shelter and inform everyone of this amazing sight. We don't want anyone to miss out. Here..." He handed over Inko and Osha's rabbit, "take this. Osha. Inko. We'll go and see the mammoths."

Now that her attention was completely diverted, Osha realised that her fears of endless walking had been silly. Up ahead, she could see where the trees gave way to the natural rock of the shelter. Grabbing Inko's hand, she turned and almost dragged him along after Grandpa.

"Hey. Hey! Osha! Slow down." Osha looked at him from under her eyelashes, slightly embarrassed by her enthusiasm.

"Sorry Inko. I just really, really, really want to see them." She slowed down and let go of his hand as she apologised again to him. Instead she walked beside him and made sure not to walk too quickly. He laughed at her as she exaggerated slowing down her pace.

In no time at all (though to Osha it felt like hours) they cleared away from the forest edge and came upon the bank of the nearby river. Both children scrambled part way up the muddy bank on their hands and knees. Ahead of them, across the water, they could see a large clearing, covered in grass.

Grandpa motioned to Osha and Inko, placing a finger to his lips. Carefully and quietly, they crept up further towards the edge of the river. The bank was high on their side and provided excellent cover for their observation.

Osha heard them before she saw them. Their large feet pounded the ground as they moved across the grassland. Once they came into view, she couldn't believe how large they were. Trees around them were dwarfed by the height of the magnificent animals. Their tusks stretched long and curled up slightly and between them, huge trunks gently swayed as they moved. Along their backs, heads and legs was a thick coat of long brown hair. They moved slowly, stopping every so often to graze on the grasses beneath their feet.

"What are they doing here?" she whispered as quietly as she could.

"Moving south I expect" came the quiet reply from Grandpa, "I just can't believe that we're seeing them. I truly didn't think there were any left around here." his voice shook with emotion and his eyes filled with tears,

"Why're you crying Grandpa?" his granddaughter asked, puzzled at his response.

"Once, not that long ago, they freely roamed these lands. We lived alongside them and sometimes they gave their lives to help us live on. Then slowly but surely, they began to disappear. We'd go seasons and then many winters before seeing them. The last time, I was a young lad. Not much older than you, Young'un and…" he stopped to wipe his damp face "I'm an old man now, Osha. I might not get to see them again." Osha shook her head. Crawling closer, she put her small arms around his waist and buried her head in his chest as she too felt tears well in her eyes. Inko stood watching them. Nothing needed to be said.

They continued to stay like this for a while longer, watching the simple lives of the mammoths. At one point, one of the animals looked almost directly at them as she lowered her long trunk into the river to collect some water.

Osha smiled at the mother and she must have realised they meant her no harm, as she didn't react with anything more than a gentle snort as she turned away.

It was the baby that Osha particularly loved. In a strange way, it reminded her of her younger brother and cousin when they were playing. The young mammoth would run up to each mammoth one at a time and try to get them to begin a chase. At one point, the playful youngster gingerly splashed into the river and began spraying water all around.

Through it all, Grandpa kept a smile on his face, but it didn't quite meet his eyes and there was little twinkle there.

The rustling sound of the approach of more people momentarily distracted them. Pira and a few others from the camp came up to meet them at the bank. The small group of people stopped and stared at the sight across the river. Osha pointed, her grin lighting up her tear stained cheeks.

"Look Pira," she whispered, "mammoths. Real, live mammoths. Aren't they amazing?" Pira clambered slowly up the same bank, her eyes still fixed on the legendary creatures, and sat so she could see them. She couldn't believe her eyes.

By this time the sun had well and truly set and the cold which had plagued them all day had become even more acute. The winds became stronger and small flakes of snow could be felt on the air.

Grandpa turned to them all and silently indicated with a movement of his head and a gesture of his hands that it was time for them to head back to the shelter. Almost as one, the small group of people stood and carefully made their way down the steep riverbank.

Osha was loath to leave the best sight she had ever had but even she could admit the wind had a very harsh edge to it. Grandpa kept looking up, his well-trained eyes showing concern about the coming storm. Once they were away from the mammoths and knew they wouldn't startle them, he hurried everyone along.

Snow and wind swirled around them as they arrived back at the shelter. Coming into their home, Osha and the others shook off the few flakes that had landed in their hair. They were grateful for the warmth of the fire burning in the hearth.

Ma too had made sure there was a good strong broth prepared and the rabbit caught by the children took pride of place nestled within the delicious, steaming meal. Osha looked forward to eating it and then, with her fatigue returning in full force, she would happily snuggle beneath warm hides and dream of the mammoths.

Chapter Fourteen

The following weeks became colder and colder as the winter fully set in. Most of the time was spent sheltering from the winds that battered the outside world. They continued to practice knapping and Pira her stitching, but the weather was not appropriate for hunting or exploring much further than the immediate vicinity of the shelter.

One particularly cold day, the children, women of the household and Grandpa were all sitting around the warm fire. Since the mammoth sighting, Grandpa's stories had centred a lot around the importance of animals, not just for hunting. Some of these stories were ones they knew well but others were new.

Osha was sitting in front of her ma who was gently braiding her hair. Inko's ma sat beside her. The more time the quiet woman spent with the family, the more she was beginning to say. Osha loved her soft, quiet voice it had a quality to it like that of the pipe.

Osha looked around as she heard Inko's ma very quietly say something,

"She deserves to know." The feel of her ma's hands on her hair grew slack and she felt a gentle tap on her shoulder. Confused, Osha looked into her ma's eyes as she moved to sit beside her on the stone bench. The rest of the adults in the room, ushered the other children further away from the two and Grandpa nodded at them both, before continuing with his story.

"I have my own tale to tell you Osha." her ma said, taking her hands into her own. Osha frowned as she saw tears beginning to form in Ma's eyes. "It is something that I should have told you long ago. But I just couldn't let myself see it happen again." She stopped and looked down at their linked hands before returning her gaze to her daughter's eyes.

"I know you have wondered who the strange man in your dreams is. You said that he looks like Polto?" Osha nodded, afraid of what Ma might say next, would she get angry? Instead, Mara continued, a small smile playing on her lips "Yes, I suppose he does. Well, you see…" she paused and swallowed, "he's your pa, Osha. His name was Pulo and I loved him very much." Osha watched as her Ma's eyes began to empty tears down her cheeks, but she didn't stop the story, "Ana has helped me see that it's time you learned what happened. You are growing up, going on adventures and learning to maybe form your own household." At this Osha grimaced and shook her head and her ma laughed,

"OK, maybe not yet, but as you grow more, you deserve to know who your pa was. Your going on that hunt with your grandpa brought it all back, but I'm not going to keep the truth from you anymore, no matter how hard it is to face. After all, I've still got you and your brothers and sister as well as Usso and his family. We are lucky." At this she stopped and looked over towards Ana who was sitting listening to Grandpa's story. Then she closed her eyes, took a deep breath and began the tale of Pulo's fate.

"One day when you had seen about one winter, he, Grandpa and Usso went on a hunt. They were out in the grasslands tracking some elk when they were attacked by a pack of wolves." She stopped, wiped her cheeks, took another breath and continued,

"Your pa saved your grandpa and uncle's lives. He distracted the wolves, making them chase him while they got away." She looked down at her hands and breathed deep again before finishing, "but he didn't survive. When they went back with more men from the band..." Osha placed a hand on her ma's she understood, she didn't need to say what had happened. Mara smiled at her, raising a hand to caress her cheek, "I'm sorry I've been so angry, Osha. It's just been very hard being without him. I want you to know that he loved you very much and he would be so, so proud of how grown up you are." Osha felt tears forming at the back of her own eyes. Without being told, she'd known that her pa wasn't alive anymore but hearing the story was difficult. She could understand why Ma hadn't told her. She looked up at her and leaned into her shoulder.

The weeks turned into months and they too passed much as the previous months had. The greatest difference was the images that Osha began to leave scrawled into as many surfaces as she could. It was a simple picture, scrubbed out several times when she couldn't quite depict the perfect proportions or more generally she just didn't think it was very good. It showed a mother mammoth and her baby playing in a river; the baby looked directly out towards the viewer. She just couldn't get it quite right.

As the winter season progressed into spring, the winds became slightly softer, the days that little bit longer and the time of their return to the summer cave became ever closer. Osha's excitement continued to grow. She counted the days until they would leave again, watching for those signs of spring which meant it would be time to make the journey.

As the weeks went on, birds could again be seen flying, their beaks laden with twigs and materials to build their nests. They watched as the valley below them blossomed and the green of new life spread, with the growth of new leaves in the forest.

The day finally arrived when it was time to set out. Osha turned to look back at their home for the previous season. "You know, it's not too bad here. The shelter protects us, and the hunting was tons of fun!" Pira and Inko nodded in agreement. It had been a good few months with many changes.

The journey was very different to the one they had taken the months before, not least because Pira was able to walk without having to be pulled on her special chair. The weather too was much warmer and although they still carried hides in case the fair weather turned to rain, the azure sky was reassuring.

Groups of people conversed together, sharing stories of the season as. happy children ran about, enjoying the freedom of the long walk after being confined for so long.

As they came upon familiar areas once again, Osha's excitement grew at the prospect of being able to visit the cave whenever she wanted. She had truly missed all the amazing images (not just Grandpa's) and the joy she would feel after seeing real mammoths herself, was almost indescribable. Beside her Pira and Inko talked about what they would do first. Osha didn't need to say where she was going.

On entering the camp, they placed their items down. The other households had moved on to find their preferred locations. It was always interesting seeing how the camp looked after being ravaged by winter.

Luckily their shelter poles remained standing and they could quickly rebuild once again. The hides were a little worse for wear after so many months, but they would do for one night. Osha helped but was very impatient to get to the cave. She roughly put things down and as quickly as possible pulled on hides and tied off ropes. Finally, they were done, and Ma indicated that she could escape to her haven.

"Osha. Wait there a minute." Grandpa walked over to her. In his hand he held a small wooden bowl. Impatiently she turned to him with a huff,

"What? I want to get to the cave Grandpa. Can't it wait?" The old man was slightly taken aback by her tone,

"Well I thought I might come with you. I was gonna give you a present to take with you, but I'll stay here if you prefer." Osha was curious, the last time Grandpa had been with her into the cave was when she was very young.

"Oh. Well that would be fine. What present?" She tried to see what was in the bowl, but he hid it behind his back.

"Not yet." He called over to Inko and Pira, who were still diligently helping their mas "You two, how about it, want to come to the cave with Osha and I?"

"Oh yeah!" the other two responded. As they ran over, Grandpa turned again to Osha and held out his hand with the strange bowl in it. Within it sat a strange mix of black powder and a liquid. In his other hand was a small reed.

"Know what this is, Young'un?" The twinkle was back in his eyes again. Osha's eyes in turn widened as she realised what his present was.

Together they entered the cave, the sunlight streaming in, illuminating the walls at the entrance. Grandpa had gathered together torches for each of them, prepared for the darkness deep in the cave. With her torch in hand and a grin on her face, Osha raced further into the cave network.

She reached the chosen wall before the others. She smiled at the beloved painting above her. This was the best spot: her mammoth would stand next to her Grandpa's. Standing in front, she could feel the meaning of the occasion as the dreamed images of her pa and Grandpa's words, from their encounter with the mammoths, rang in her head.

The rest of the group came up quietly behind her, they had known where she would be.

Silently, Grandpa handed her the bowl which contained the charcoal pigment. Turning to the wall, the cave towered high above her head, but she wasn't afraid: Grandpa, Pira and Inko stood behind her and she finally knew exactly what she was going to do. This time she would get it right.

Grandpa lifted her up so that she could reach higher up the wall. Brush in hand, she began painting the most important picture of her life.

Finally, the mammoths would stand proud, calling to the future from that cave wall, once again.

<u>Glossary</u>

Ancestors   People in your family that lived long before you were born.

Band   The large group of people who lived together in the same area during the Stone Age. Made up of several different households.

Fire-hardened   Burned in a fire to make it easier to light.

Flax   A natural material that could be used for thread. Used to make rope and tie things together.

Flint   A type of layered rock used to make blades and other sharp items.

Flint core   The natural rock from which blades are made

Gesture   The movement of hands instead of words

Hammer stone   The large, hard stone used to hit the flint in knapping.

Hearth   A fire.

Hide   The skin from an animal used to make clothes and other useful items.

Hilt   The handle of a blade.

Households	The groups that make up a band. They live together in a single camp. Usually related to each other.
Knapping	To shape a piece of stone by hitting it, breaking off flakes to use as blades.
Moon cycles	Months. Follows the changes in the moon.
Oral history	Stories told by speaking rather than writing. A common way of learning before writing.
Pressure-flake	Using a bone or stone to chip off small pieces at the edge of a blade to add serrations.
Pigment	Paint made from natural materials.
Seasons	The groups of months that mark the change of weather – Spring, Summer, Autumn, Winter.
Serration	Saw or tooth-like edge on a blade.
Shards	Tiny, sharp pieces of materials
Spirits	Belief in the natural energy of the Earth/ancestors/gods which underlies life.
Tunic	A long shirt-like piece of clothing which was made from animal hide.

Upper-Paleolithic   The period of time before Stone Age people began to farm. People lived in temporary shelters and moved around.

Winters   Years. Follows how many winters have passed. Someone who has 'seen eight winters' is eight or nine years old, depending on when they were born.

Become a Source Detective

If you have enjoyed

From the Cave Wall: A Stone Age Story

go to **www.jgjbooks.com** and

Become a Source Detective

A completely **free** reader's club.

Every member receives a welcome message from the author and a **free** copy of the exclusive e-book:

Behind the Cave Wall

Learn more about Osha's World!

Discover writing secrets!

Explore the history of the Upper Paleolithic!

Printed in Great Britain
by Amazon